THE 11TH HOUR

THE 11TH HOUR

KRISTINE SCARROW

DUNDURN
TORONTO

Cover image: shutterstock.com/Tom Tom
Printer: Webcom

Library and Archives Canada Cataloguing in Publication

Scarrow, Kristine, author
    The 11th hour / Kristine Scarrow.

Issued in print and electronic formats.
ISBN 978-1-4597-4037-2 (softcover).--ISBN 978-1-4597-4038-9 (PDF).--ISBN 978-1-4597-4039-6 (EPUB)

    I. Title. II. Title: Eleventh hour.

PS8637.C27E43 2018   jC813'.6   C2017-904456-7
                                              C2017-904457-5

1 2 3 4 5   22   21   20   19   18

We acknowledge the support of the **Canada Council for the Arts**, which last year invested $153 million to bring the arts to Canadians throughout the country, and the **Ontario Arts Council** for our publishing program. We also acknowledge the financial support of the **Government of Ontario**, through the **Ontario Book Publishing Tax Credit** and the **Ontario Media Development Corporation**, and the **Government of Canada**.

Nous remercions le **Conseil des arts du Canada** de son soutien. L'an dernier, le Conseil a investi 153 millions de dollars pour mettre de l'art dans la vie des Canadiennes et des Canadiens de tout le pays.

Care has been taken to trace the ownership of copyright material used in this book. The author and the publisher welcome any information enabling them to rectify any references or credits in subsequent editions.

— *J. Kirk Howard, President*

The publisher is not responsible for websites or their content unless they are owned by the publisher.

Printed and bound in Canada.

VISIT US AT

🌐 dundurn.com | 🐦 @dundurnpress | 📘 dundurnpress | 📷 dundurnpress

Dundurn
3 Church Street, Suite 500
Toronto, Ontario, Canada

M5E 1M2

To D, M, and R:
Sometimes a family has to break in order for its members to become whole again, but a broken family is still a family that loved. Whether it's in this life or the next, the hope is that one day it will mend back into something beautiful.

"Crawl inside this body — find me where I am most ruined, love me *there* …"

— Rune Lazuli

"At the root of this dilemma is the way we view mental health.… Whether an illness affects your heart, your leg, or your brain, it's still an illness, and there should be no distinction …"

— Michelle Obama

6:00 A.M.

ANNIKA

The clock's large red numbers glow 6:02 a.m. I must've missed the alarm. It was set for five thirty; sometimes I sleep through it and it beeps for ten minutes straight before giving up on me and going silent again. Any other day this would be fine, but this morning the rest of my family *must* still be asleep, oblivious to the plans for my day.

I listen for any signs of life in the house but hear nothing. My terrier, Roxy, is nestled in bed with me as usual. I ruffle the top of her head and her ears. She rests her head against my rib cage and my throat gets thick at the thought of leaving her behind. I can't take her with me though. The plan is for Dylan to pick me up after I let Roxy outside, that way she won't bark and try to follow me out of the house. When I let her out in the morning, she quickly pees and then stretches out on the patio, enjoying the morning sun. We usually leave her out there until she barks to come in, which is at least a half-hour later, and by then I should be long gone.

I went to bed at ten last night. Way earlier than normal for a Friday night — especially since it's family movie night and we usually don't get started until late in the evening, but the plans for the day had me restless and I couldn't seem to focus on anything but what we were going to do.

"You feeling okay, sweetie?" my mom had asked. "You're still coughing." I'd had this cough and cold for a couple of weeks now. Although I wasn't feeling great, I was thankful for the diversion. I could just say I was sick and head to my room to finish all the last-minute preparations.

"Yeah, I'm good," I assured her. "Just tired. I think I'm going to head to bed early."

Dad entered the room with a large bowl of popcorn and a stack of napkins. My twelve-year-old brother Mark was waiting for us to join him, his hand on the remote control. The opening credits of a movie were on the TV screen and everyone was about to settle in to watch it together.

"Annika, you're not going to watch the movie with us?" Disappointment washed over him. I rolled my eyes a bit. I was seventeen years old and Dad still wanted me to be his little girl, joining in excitedly on any family activity. He'd be happy if I was still coming over for movie night at forty. Mom came toward me and kissed me on the forehead.

"You feel a bit warm, honey," she said.

"Nah, I'm good," I assured her. "I just need some sleep."

Mom stared at me for a moment. "Maybe we should check your temperature?"

"I'm sure it's fine," I said, brushing her off.

"Okay, well, get some sleep and if you need anything …"

"Yeah, I know. Thanks, Mom."

"See you in the morning." I'd already left the room, and her parting words cut through me. I wouldn't see her in the morning. Little did she know that if everything went as planned, I'd be long gone before the rest of my family woke for the day. The truth was I didn't know when I'd see them again. Although I was excited for the adventure before Dylan and me, leaving my family behind made me ache.

The last few months had gotten really rocky between us though, and I knew they wouldn't understand. They wanted to keep me from the very thing I wanted the most — a future with Dylan.

When I got to my room, I quickly shut the door behind me and got down on my hands and knees to pull the backpack out from under my bed. It was bulging, the zipper barely able to close. How do you know what to pack when you're about to walk out of your life as you know it? What do you take when you're making a new life with someone you love, but when doing so means leaving everything you've ever known behind?

My phone vibrated. It was Dylan, texting me.

can't wait for tomorrow. love u babe. 9:52 p.m.

I reply:

Love you too. 9:53 p.m.

My heart surged at his words. I could feel his excitement through the phone. Dylan is such a passionate guy, always wearing his heart on his sleeve and coming up with grand ideas for our life together. He gives so much to everything he wants to do that his enthusiasm is contagious.

I know we'll have a good life together — that he loves me more than anything.

I pressed my hand to my forehead — I supposed I did feel a bit warm. Maybe trying to get a good night's sleep would be the best thing for me, so I could wake feeling energetic and ready for the day. I shoved my backpack back under my bed and did a last-minute swoop of my room for anything I might want to bring. I shivered as I studied my room and drank in all of its contents. I rubbed my arms, my heart heavy. This nine-by-ten-foot room that had been my haven for all of my seventeen years, with its pale yellow walls and flowery bedspread. The lace curtain panels on either side of my window, which I had requested from my grandmother's house after she passed. Bits of scotch tape remained on my walls from when I had posters hung up. I still had posters of Adam Levine (my celebrity crush) and Bruno Mars (my favourite singer) but I'd long removed the others, thinking I was getting too old to have posters tacked on my walls, covering them like wallpaper. My bulletin board had ticket stubs from the concerts I'd been to, a photo of me holding car keys in the air (the day I got my licence), and the honour roll certificates I'd received for grades nine, ten, and eleven. The shelves above my desk held my soccer trophies going back to when I was little, and my two favourite stuffies — LuLu, a honey-coloured bear with only one eye and half of the stuffing missing that I'd had since I was two, and a plush neon-pink smiley face with dangly arms and legs that Dylan had won for me at the fair.

I'd miss this room. Maybe we'd get settled somewhere and Mom and Dad would warm to the idea of Dylan again, see that we really loved each other and that we'd be staying together for good. Then we could visit and I'd get to see my other things again.

I settled into my bed, cuddled into my comforter, and wiped a tear from my cheek. Although I couldn't wait to start a life with Dylan, I couldn't help but feel sad at what I was leaving behind. If only my parents had a different opinion of Dylan. If only they supported us being together, then we wouldn't have felt like we had to run away.

My phone vibrates at 6:05 a.m. Another text from Dylan. This time it's a photo of the two of us that Dylan took on the Ferris wheel at the fair. My long dark hair is blowing softly in the breeze, the lights of the amusement park and the city glowing behind us. Dylan has his other arm around me, pulling me close, and he's kissing my cheek. I'm smiling from ear to ear, feeling every ounce of his love in that moment. This is why I'm leaving. Because Dylan makes me feel like no one else. Because Dylan loves me. Because Dylan is my future.

I brush my hair and pull it back into a ponytail and only pull my hair halfway through the last twist of the elastic. I apply a bit of eyeshadow and blush and my signature lip gloss — shell pink, it's called. Knowing we'll be in the car for a long time, I decide on black yoga pants and my Aeropostale hoodie. It's all about comfort today.

My heart flutters a bit at the thought of being alone with Dylan for so long. Even though we've been dating for six months already, we've really only been able to see each other for a couple of hours at a time. I usually have a few shifts a week at Shoppers Drug Mart and then there's cheerleading practice and dance — well, that is until I quit a couple of months ago. My parents were so upset when they found out I wasn't going to go anymore.

"You've been dancing since you were three!" my mom practically shrieked. "You *love* to dance!" Both of them looked at me in shock, as though I'd just announced that I'd murdered someone or something. And then telling them that cheerleading came next didn't go any better.

"I don't know what the heck is going on here, but I just don't get it." My dad had sat at the table, his hands massaging his temples. "Why would you give these things up?"

I missed Dylan a lot. My part-time job, dance, and cheerleading took up a lot of time, and we wanted to be together more. And the more time I spent with Dylan, the more I'd started drifting away from my friends at the same time. It's like we started growing apart. Ali and Tara, my two closest friends since kindergarten who also danced with me and helped lead the cheerleading team, seemed more preoccupied with winning the cheer competition again than anything else, and I just lost interest. I still loved the competition, the practice to get everything in perfect synch, the thrill of landing an incredible stunt — but it felt like the commitment was getting to be too much.

Having more time with Dylan is all I want. No one knows yet, but I've also quit my job. Dylan and I will be a long way from home.

DYLAN

We're finally doing it. After all of our talking about it, it's actually happening. We can get away from this damn place and start over somewhere else. I'm so tired of everyone being on my back, how no one really understands me. No one but Annika.

Annika's the best thing to happen to me. She's everything I've ever wanted in a girl. Since the first day I saw her I knew she was the one for me. I've never been one for casual dating. I've always held out for the girl who blows my mind right off the bat. You know, love at first sight.

I'm only eighteen and the thing is — I already know that I'm going to marry her. I've never met anyone like her. She's gorgeous, smart, sexy, and kind. She's the total package, and at times I wonder how I ever got someone like her in the first place.

Yes, I've said it — she's too good for me. I don't deserve her. I mean, look at her. She's every guy's dream and she chose me. *Me*. It still shocks me. It's not that I'm not a catch myself; it's just that Annika is on a whole other level that I can't match. Probably no guy could. I'm a pretty good-looking guy — I mean I've never had any problems trying to find a girl to date. There are usually line-ups of giggling girls practically tripping over themselves to talk to me after my basketball games. I know it's high-school basketball and not the NBA, but I'm kind of a big deal for our school. As the top scorer on the team, I know how it's done.

It's going to be hard for Anni to leave her family. I know it's been weighing on her and that's why it's taken so long to get to this point. It won't be a problem for me though. The faster I get away from my parents and my job (well, technically I don't have it anymore) and everything else, the better.

My bags were packed weeks ago, and I barely gave my house a glance before loading up and racing to get Annika. I don't want her to change her mind, to decide that we should stick around after all. The thought of us being alone for hours on end, with no one interfering with us, excites me like you wouldn't believe. She's my future and I'm ready for it.

We'll get settled up there, far enough from everyone. I can't wait. I'll fish and hunt for us. I'll teach her how, too, and the two of us will be a team. We'll have fires at night and we'll stare up at the stars. Annika loves animals. I'll find us a dog — a pup from a farm litter, perhaps — and she won't miss Roxy as much because we'll have a new little family member of our own. I'll surprise her with it when she least expects it. She'll light up and gush over the pup. The way she'll look at me, so excited and thankful, I can't wait. I'll do whatever I can to make her happy. I know she'll love this life.

I pull up to her neighbour's house, careful to position my car away from the living room window. The last thing we need is her dad coming out asking questions. He'd be suspicious for sure. We wouldn't be heading anywhere after that. Her parents would stand over us, telling us we'd be staying put. I can picture her dad saying something completely over the top like, "Over my dead body!" and pulling Annika behind him as though I was dangerous.

It didn't start out like this. In fact, we used to hang out together — until they started thinking I was a bad influence on Annika, and then their opinion of me changed pretty quickly.

Her dad has this way of looking at me. His eyebrows raise and his lips purse together as though he's studying me carefully, trying to get a handle on me. I always greet him with a "Hi, Mr. Dietty" when I see him and I've been nothing but completely respectful. All I want is for them to do the same for me. You'd think they'd see how happy their daughter is and be happy for us; instead they're trying to keep us apart.

Her parents are real strict — maybe even more so since we've been dating. They've even forbidden us from seeing each other now, but nothing is going to break us apart. They can't see that they are part of the reason we want to leave. They have no idea how they're driving their own daughter away. Maybe once we're gone they'll take a hard look at their behaviour and they'll begin to understand where we're coming from.

My heart is pounding knowing that Annika will have to slip out undetected for this to work. I pull out my phone to text her and let her know I'm here. It's go time.

7:00 A.M.

U ready? 7:02 a.m.

    Yes. 7:02 a.m.

    I'm outside. 7:02 a.m.

I go to the window, and sure enough his two-door black hatchback is in front of our neighbour's house, just far enough from view from our living room window.

    Be right there. 7:03 a.m.

I guess this is it. I swing the backpack up over my shoulders and it lands with a thud against my back, almost winding me. I survey the room one last time, tears welling up again. But as hard as it is to say goodbye, I am excited to see Dylan.

If my parents wake up, I don't know what I'll do. They'd absolutely flip out if they had any idea what we were planning. They didn't always hate Dylan. The first time I brought him over, my dad shook his hand and welcomed him in. My brother joined the two of them and they sat and watched baseball on TV. My mom made them nachos and put out bowls of chips and dip and I was thrilled that they were accepting him. Dylan made my dad laugh several times, and by the end of it, it felt like he'd been around forever. Dylan kept dropping by, and at first, my parents didn't seem to think there was any problem with it.

As the weeks went on, though, they were less and less supportive of our relationship.

"Maybe you should spend a little less time with Dylan," my mom said one evening.

"Why?" I sounded defensive, but it was hard not to.

"You just seem to be focusing all of your attention on him instead of your friends or your activities. It's not like you."

It's not like I'd ditched everything to be with him. It's just that I didn't care about those things as much anymore. Dylan was everything I needed.

"Maybe those things don't interest me as much anymore," I told her.

"Maybe they should. I'm not saying Dylan is a bad guy — we like him! I'm just saying that we're concerned about some of the choices you're making."

"You can't decide how I spend my time. I'm not a little kid anymore."

"No, but when we see that you're not even acting like the person we know, we have a right to be concerned."

"So, what? You have no faith in me? You guys can't control my life forever. And Dylan makes me happy. Happier than I've ever been."

My mom stared at me with such exasperation and disappointment that I wanted to scream. I wasn't hurting anybody. Didn't they remember what it was like to fall in love?

The ball game–watching stopped; the friendly handshakes and well-wishes at the door stopped as well. I started running out to meet Dylan before he could reach the front door, and eventually he preferred to stay in the car than face my parents, too.

I decided to invite Dylan for dinner so that I could try to patch things between him and my parents, but then things went downhill even further. In fact, they've basically forbidden me to spend time with him now. But we're still together, stronger than ever. I think back to that dinner and how Dylan said all the right things (or at least I thought he did), but my dad kept interrogating him.

"If you're a responsible young man, then why is Annika coming home so late?"

"If you care about this girl, why are you letting her quit all of the activities that she's worked hard at and loved her whole life?"

"Do you think jeopardizing Annika's future by having her work fewer shifts at her job is a good idea? Because it seems she'd rather spend the time with you. What else would you like her to give up?"

I kept yelling, "DAD!" but he wouldn't stop. My mom just sat there quietly. She wouldn't stick up for me. By remaining quiet, she showed she was in agreement with everything he said.

I fought back. "Those things have nothing to do with Dylan. I made those choices!"

"So you're influencing my daughter to make dumb choices then …" My dad's eyes bore into Dylan. I could see Dylan trying to remain calm. He kept whispering that it was okay, that he could handle this, but this was not how I wanted things to go. I wanted to spend more time with Dylan. And he wanted that, too. We were falling in love — didn't my dad know what that was like? My parents wouldn't be able to control my life forever. Didn't they know they were driving me away talking like this?

The night was a disaster. And even though Dylan was polite and calm during the entire ordeal, I knew he was upset. It wasn't until we were back outside and I was saying bye to him that I truly saw how much it had affected him.

"I'm so sorry, Dyl!" I told him. I held his hands and caressed the tops of his knuckles with my fingers. "They'll come around."

"I don't think they will," Dylan muttered. He was shaking his head and his whole body stood rigidly. "I didn't expect your dad to be such a jerk."

"Me neither. Honest. If I knew he'd be like that, I wouldn't have had this dinner in the first place."

"Well, you're almost an adult, Anni. They're going to have to get used to it."

"We'll give it some time. Eventually they won't be able to help but love you too."

My parents had come to the doorway.

"Say goodbye, Annika." My dad's voice boomed. I quickly kissed Dylan on the cheek and watched him as he walked to his car.

"Thanks again for having me for dinner, Mr. and Mrs. Dietty," Dylan called politely. "That was a delicious meal, Mrs. Dietty!" They said nothing in return.

I waved to Dylan as he drove off. I stormed back into the house.

"You're practically throwing your life away these days," my mom said. "All over a boy? A boy with no goals? If he loved you, he'd be supporting you in all the things you love to do."

"Did it ever occur to you guys that maybe I don't want to dance or cheer anymore for my own reasons? Reasons that have nothing to do with Dylan?"

"Your whole behaviour has changed since you two got involved," my mom pointed out. "You're studying less, missing curfew, getting grounded, ditching your friends, and quitting things left and right. How else are we supposed to react?"

"You aren't even giving him a chance. You guys treated him terribly tonight."

"We don't want you seeing him any longer," my dad stated matter-of-factly.

"WHAT?!" I screamed. "How can you say that?! You're punishing him for my choices!"

But the discussion was over. My parents went up to their bedroom and shut the door, signalling that they were retiring for the night. I immediately called Dylan to apologize again. I hoped that it wouldn't change how he felt about me. Luckily it didn't.

I adjust my backpack and turn my bedroom door handle slowly and carefully. I open the door and creep down the empty hallway, then make a dash down our carpeted stairs, grateful for the sound-muffling padding. Roxy follows dutifully on my heels. I'm careful to bypass the third step from the bottom, the creaky one, and when I reach the main floor of the house I let out my breath in one long puff of air. The lights are all off, the curtains and blinds still closed. Only the early-morning sunlight finds its way through small crevices. Everyone is still asleep. I take a quick look around, second-guess whether or not I should have written a note (I didn't), and then I let Roxy out the back door as though it's any other morning. I decide to join Dylan before someone sees or hears me leave.

I turn the front door handle slowly and pull the door open as quietly as I can, but it creaks loudly. I squeeze myself through as best as I can without opening it any farther. I pull it closed behind me and then bolt off of the front porch toward Dylan's car.

His face is lit up like never before. He's grinning from ear to ear, his longer curly locks blocking part of his face. One look at that boyish grin of his and I want to melt. He's so handsome. He opens the trunk for me and reaches for my backpack. I take it off of my shoulders and pass it to him. The car is pretty full. I see a large duffle bag, blankets, pillows, bags of food. He's come prepared.

"Hey, beautiful," he says. He pulls me into him and we kiss passionately. My heart hammers in my ears; that's how strong my blood pumps at his touch. I'm breathless when we pull away. I don't want to stop, but we can't stand in the street kissing all day. We've got to get out of here before we're found out. Now that we'll be living on our own, I'll be able to be with him in ways I've only dreamed of.

"I'm so excited!" I say back. He's got a twinkle in his eye.

"Looks like we're all set."

"Let's get out of here!" I reply, and he laughs.

We get into the car and the moment my seat-belt clicks Dylan pulls away. He grabs my hand and squeezes it, stealing playful glances my way every chance he gets. When we're a few blocks away, he pulls over.

"What's going on?"

Dylan reaches behind my seat for something and then surprises me with a bouquet of sunflowers.

"They're beautiful!"

"Your favourite," he says. "They've got nothing on you, babe."

Sunflowers have always intrigued me — the way they continually turn toward the sun as though they always want to experience warmth and happiness. I love how Dylan knows just what I love and how he always tries to make me happy.

"Are we really doing this?" I ask. We've been talking about this for about two months. At first I thought it was just a pipe dream, something we talked about as a "wouldn't this be cool?"–type scenario, but then I realized Dylan was serious. He'd just finished high school in June and was ready for something different. His part-time job with his uncle's construction company wasn't going so well. Dylan said his uncle was impossible to work for — demanding and unfair. They'd had a few heated arguments in the last few months and Dylan had walked off the job more than once.

"I can't take it anymore," he said to me the last time. "He takes advantage of me because I'm family. And he can't see it. Half the time he doesn't even know what he's doing anyhow. I could probably work circles around him if he let me run it."

I had never met his uncle, but he sounded like a jerk. With my parents trying to keep us apart and Dylan having problems at work, it seems like a perfect time to leave. We'll get a fresh start, somewhere far away from everyone. I won't have to keep sneaking out to see Dylan and we'll be able to spend all of our time together.

"Watch, Annika, we'll get settled up north and I'll start my own business. We'll be rolling in it in no time." I know Dylan's relieved to be moving on from the whole situation.

"We're doing this," he says loudly, as though he can't quite believe it himself, and squeezes my hand. I look back to the packed car and my stomach jumps excitedly. I wonder what it'll be like, actually living with someone besides my family. I picture us waking up in the morning, him giving me a sweet kiss and bringing me coffee. We'll listen to the birds outside the window and figure out how to spend the day.

"It should take us about three hours to get there," Dylan says. We're headed north to Delaronde Lake, by Big River, to his family's cabin. It's the perfect place for us to go because, since his parents' divorce five years ago, no one has used it.

"My parents are happy someone will finally be using the cabin," Dylan tells me.

"They know we're going?" I'm surprised. I thought this was a secret from everyone.

"Of course. I had to get the key somehow."

Dylan's parents are a lot more lax than mine. He can pretty well do whatever he wants. His mom lives on the other side of the country and is remarried. Dylan barely talks to her. He thinks her new husband is a loser. She's pregnant too — and he isn't crazy about having such a big age gap between him and his new sibling. His dad owns his own business and is gone all of the time, even more so since the divorce. Dylan says his dad goes out to the bar with his friends and tries to live like he's twenty again, which is pretty ridiculous when you're forty-five.

It must be nice to have parents who let you do what you want. Who trust you. Mine seem to follow my every move. They're always asking questions, texting and phoning to see where I am. If they would just back off, I wouldn't be in this car on this road.

"You're going to love this place!" Dylan says. "The first thing we're doing is going fishing."

I smile. Dylan loves to fish. He sometimes takes his rod and reel and his tackle box and drives down to Eagle Creek or Blackstrap Provincial Park to fish for the day. His dad taught him to fish when he was a little boy.

"Anni, there's something about being out on the water. You're going to love it."

I'm not particularly into the idea of catching fish, let alone having to touch them, but I know how much this means to Dylan so I want to give it a try. My own family goes camping every year but we never fish.

"There's a boat up there?" I ask.

"Sure," Dylan says. "Best time to go is early in the morning. The water is so calm — like glass. Or we can go at sunset and watch the sun go down together." He winks at me. The thought of sitting in the boat together at sunset, the water glistening all around us, is dreamy.

"I packed up a cooler and went grocery shopping last night," Dylan says. "We've got a good load of food for the next couple of weeks."

Wow. He's really planned this out and gotten everything together.

"I was thinking — we could have hotdogs cooked on an open fire tonight."

"Those are the best," I agree. "I like mine burnt and crispy."

"Anni?" Dylan says. I look over at him, at his eyes sparkly and lit up like vivid stars.

"I love you." And once again my heart feels ready to explode. This is why I will follow Dylan to the ends of the earth.

Dylan picks up speed as we pass the last set of street lights in the city. Now, there is little more than open road before us. I clap my hands and giggle.

"Goodbye, Saskatoon." I wave back at the city behind us. It's going to be a hot day; it's warm already. The open prairie comes into view — a sight that never fails to thrill me. The landscape is full of colour — rich greens, the tawny colour of wheat, and mustard-yellow patches dot the horizon as far as the eye can see. Lots of people poke fun at this province for its perpetually flat terrain. They joke that you could watch your dog run away for miles, but I love it. I love how the flat land makes it easier to see the incredible sky. In fact, that's our province's tagline: *Land of the Living Skies*. We have breathtaking sunrises and sunsets.

"We'll probably be able to see the northern lights better out there too, won't we?" I ask.

"You bet we will. We'll take a blanket down to the shore and watch from there!"

"I can't wait!" I've always loved the sky.

I take in our surroundings. It's beautiful and life feels so full of possibility. A tickle in my throat makes me cough, and it takes me a couple of minutes to regain my composure.

"Still sick?"

"I'm okay," I say, but in reality my body feels tired and sore from coughing so much. But nothing is going to get in the way of this perfect day and the promise it holds.

DYLAN

We've done it. The weather is beautiful, the radio is playing some of my favourite songs. It's like everything is coming together perfect. Anni's not feeling so hot though, I can tell by how quiet she is. I hope it's not because she's sad or worried about what we're doing. I can take care of everything. We don't need other people. We'll be just fine on our own.

I look over at my girl, at how the sun's rays are highlighting the side of her head. Her rich brown hair gleams in the sunlight. I want to reach out and touch it and feel the silkiness in my fingers. She's stretching in her seat, and I can't help but glance at her figure. God, she's gorgeous. I want her. I want her so badly it hurts.

She slips off her sandals and places her feet on the dash. I want to tell her to get them off, that I've just wiped the whole car down and even buffed the dash. Her feet might leave marks, and seriously, who wants sweaty, dirty feet right near the air vents and on their nice, clean dashboard? But she looks so good, so happy, I decide to let it go.

She stretches her legs even farther, until her feet touch the windshield. I can't concentrate on the road with her legs outstretched. I want to stare at them instead. Her feet leave smudge marks on the glass, and she giggles.

"Can you put your legs down?" I ask her nicely. Besides the visual distraction, which is actually quite fantastic, I really can't handle her feet messing up my car.

"You don't like them up here?" she teases, smudging her side of the windshield even more with her toes.

"Seriously, Anni. Come on!"

"I like them up here. I'm stretching," she says.

"Well, I don't! You're going to make it so I can't see anything, and it's gross."

I can see her smiling at me as though this is a big joke, but I'm serious. I want her to put her feet down.

"Is this better?" She laughs as her foot comes up toward me instead.

I swat at her foot and I know I should try to laugh, but I'm irritated and I'm going to drive this car off of the road if she keeps fooling around.

"Cut it out, Anni." My voice is harder than I intend.

"Fine," she says, pouting. "You're no fun." She lowers her legs.

Then she starts coughing, this loud, drawn-out, barking cough that ends with a choke and a gag and her face and body looking completely winded and worn. It's terrible, and I immediately feel awful for even thinking of her feet on the dash. In fact, I'll do anything to get her smile back.

Things will be better once we get there. I'll make her some tea and I'll put honey in it like my mom used to do for me when I was little. I'll chop some wood and get things ready for us. With the leaves already starting to fall, it won't be long before the cold weather sets in and we'll need to be ready for winter.

Annika's worried about how we'll stay afloat, but we'll be fine. I've got mad reno skills and cabins always need fix-ups and maintenance. It's harder to find tradespeople in rural areas so I'll be in high demand. Even though I'm not a tradesperson per se, I know my stuff and I can do just as good a job as any of them. I'm sure I'll be able to build a business in no time.

Working for myself will be great. I won't have anyone monitoring my every move and criticizing my work. I was working for my Uncle Bill and I learned that you should never work for family. He was condescending right from the beginning; analyzing my work and making me feel disrespected. He walked around like he was some big-time hotshot know-it-all, and that I should be forever indebted to him for giving me a job.

He didn't allow me a lot of time off, so I decided to show up when I felt like it. Some people need to be taught how to treat others, and he needed to know that he couldn't get away with treating me like a lowly servant.

He pulled me aside a couple of weeks ago. "Dylan, if you can't come into work on time, I'll have to give your position to someone else." I smirked. He wouldn't be able to replace me.

The other guys on the crew were good guys, and they didn't seem to have the same issues that I had. My uncle had called me out in front of them many times, and all I could think was how he needed to learn a lesson on respect.

We were finishing a tile floor in a commercial building. We'd already done it once, but my uncle wasn't happy with it. He said it was uneven and poorly done and we had to jackhammer it up. None of us were happy about redoing it.

I was spacing the tile; we'd be adding the grout soon. I'd been on my knees all day, and I was dripping with sweat. It was a hot day and the air conditioning wasn't hooked up. We were all getting tired. I wanted to lighten the mood so I decided to take a can of spray paint and have a game of hangman on the plywood wall beside us. I drew the guillotine and the spaces for the letters on the wall in fluorescent pink. It was a four-word phrase.

"Okay, folks," I said in my best game show host voice. "Winner gets to skip clean-up."

The guys looked up in surprise and started laughing.

"Todd, you're up," I called out.

"R," Todd called out.

"Sorry," I said in the same game show voice. If we were going to play, we were going to make it sound like the real thing. I drew a hat on the wall, and got a few chuckles.

"Mark?"

"S," Mark said.

I added the S so it looked like this: _ _ _ _ _ S _ _ _ SS _ _ _ _

I danced a little jig and the guys clapped and hollered. This game was just what we needed to turn this day around.

"L," Cam said, rubbing his hands together expectantly.

"Yup, folks, there is an L!"

"H," Aaron called.

"We have an H, folks!" I exclaimed. I did the jig again.

"T!" Bryan said next. The guys were clearly into the game. What's work if you can't have a little fun?

"No T." I drew a circle for the face.

"Boo!" Bryan yelled back. Everyone was laughing.

"A!" We were back to Todd.

Now the puzzle looked like this: _ _ LL _ _ A_ ASSH _ L _

A couple of the guys started to shift a bit. Luke and Aaron picked up some tiles and started focusing on the floor again.

"Hey guys, whatcha doing? We're in the middle of a game here!"

They were smiling, but they looked uncomfortable. It was time to get them back into the game.

"Come on … winner misses clean-up and I'll buy them lunch tomorrow."

"I'm out," Todd told me. "Let's finish up this floor."

"What — can't have a little fun?" I said in a baby voice. My lips puckered out at him. The other guys laughed.

"Who's next? You don't give up, do you?" This was too fun to stop now.

"Dylan!" The familiar grating voice I'd grown so used to hearing since I'd started this job. It was my uncle, standing at the entrance of the building, holding a tray of Tim Hortons coffees. "What the hell are you doing?"

The other guys put their heads down and got straight to work again.

"Oh good. You're just in time. We're on coffee break right now." I laughed.

He handed coffees to the other guys and then sauntered over to me. His face was red and pinched, his breath laboured. He was mad, madder than I'd ever seen him.

"Want to solve the puzzle?" I challenged. "You leave us in this hot building all day redoing a floor that was perfectly fine and you don't think we should have a break?"

"Spray paint, Dylan? Really?"

"There'll be tile on that wall soon enough. It'll all be covered."

"I think you've gone too far this time, Dylan." My uncle was practically vibrating. It made me want to laugh. "I no longer require your services."

"What? You want to fire me?" I said, laughing. I looked at the other guys, but they were focused on the floor. None of them would make eye contact.

"Fine. This job is shit anyway!" I yelled. "But let's solve the puzzle first." I returned to my game show voice. I filled in the letters with the spray paint so that they were clear as day.

It read: BILL IS AN ASSHOLE.

"Sorry you weren't a winner," I muttered to everyone. I dropped the can of paint. It made a loud clanking sound against the ceramic tile.

That was my last day on the job and I haven't missed it one bit. I was more than ready to work for myself anyway. Some people just don't have a sense of humour.

8:00 A.M.

ANNIKA

I'm eating an orange and tearing off slices for Dylan as he drives. The juice runs down our chins at times and we laugh at each other. The vitamin C will be good for me. I'm feeling worse, but it's probably because I didn't sleep well. I've taken my inhaler again, and I'm hoping that it gives me some relief from the cough that seems to plague me.

I've had asthma since I was three. Usually I have it pretty well managed and it doesn't really affect me too much. After all, I played soccer for years and danced and made the cheerleading squad. Sometimes when I catch a cold or some other virus though, it seems to flare up and give me trouble. I threw a couple of inhalers in my purse before I left home, but at this rate my medicine is going to run out fast unless I start feeling better.

Ed Sheeran comes on the radio, and I crank it up and sing along. We're going to grow old together just like the song. And as though he knows what I'm thinking, Dylan turns down the volume a bit.

"We should get married."

"What?!"

"Us. We should get married." He says it so matter-of-factly that my jaw hangs open. "Not right now, but maybe in a year or two."

I don't know why I find this surprising; sure, I'm only seventeen, but I've already decided to spend my life with Dylan. We've made all of these plans. I guess I should've known he'd have marriage on the brain. Somehow I hadn't considered it, but maybe it's not so crazy. My parents were only nineteen when they got married, and now they've been married for nineteen years.

"I at least have to be eighteen," I say, laughing. "Is this a proposal?"

"Don't worry, Anni. When the time comes, I'll do it right."

I smile and gaze at him with love. Of course he will. Dylan's motto is *go big or go home*, and he lives large with everything he does. When he takes me out to dinner, it's to the fanciest place he can find. On special occasions he lavishes me with gifts and when we're out with friends he tries to pay for everyone. He's the most generous person I know. And when he sets his mind to something, he always finds a way to make it happen. Like when he went on a weekend trip with his friends to the mountains and they went hiking. It wasn't enough to just walk the trail — Dylan climbed a peak outside of the marked path and then jumped from the cliff into the pool of spring water below. He sent me pictures from his friend's phone. No one else had the guts to do it. He'll try anything once and lives like there's no tomorrow.

It's something I admire. I'm always so serious. I'm a major rule follower and people pleaser and I don't like to take risks. Being with Dylan has made me grow as a person; I'm trying so many new things. He's opening me up to how life can be beyond my previously boring, routine existence. I picture our future never having a dull moment.

After I have another coughing fit, Dylan brakes and steers the car to the shoulder of the highway.

"What are you doing?" I ask, alarmed.

When the car comes to a complete stop, Dylan puts it in park and opens his car door. A semi zooms past us and Dylan's hair stands on end from the force of the wind. I sit up straighter in my seat. Dylan flips the driver's seat forward to get access to the back. He pulls out a blanket and pillow and pushes his seat back into place.

He comes around to my door, opens it, and lays the blanket across me gently.

"Here's a pillow too," he says. "Try and take a nap. Maybe you'll feel better when you wake up."

"Thanks, hon," I say, touched that he'd think of doing that for me. I reach for his hand and squeeze it. His fingers interlaced with mine make me tingle.

Once we're back at highway speed, I try to shut my eyes and nap.

———

I listen to the wind and the hum of the motor as we drive, hoping it lulls me to sleep. Instead I think of everyone back home — of how surprised they'll be when they realize I'm gone. Will Ali and Tara even care? We're barely talking anymore and I didn't share our plans with them. They'll have no idea where I am.

They're not huge fans of Dylan for some reason. I've never really figured out why. I don't think it's for any one thing — I just started spending more of my free time with Dylan and I think it made them upset. Then I skipped a couple of practices, and Ali called a team meeting and the squad confronted me.

"Isn't this competition important to you, Annika? We can't practise the routines properly if you're not here."

I tried telling them that I'd had an important appointment the last time, but Tara piped up and said that her sister saw me at Dairy Queen eating ice cream with Dylan.

"Either you want to be here or you don't. But don't waste our time if you don't," Ali said. She picked up her bag and stormed out of the gym, letting the door slam behind her. I felt everyone's disapproving stares.

"What's up with you anyway?" Tara asked. The others nodded and murmured, waiting for an answer.

"Nothing," I said, shrugging.

"No, you're different," Tara said. "And I don't mean that in a good way."

As if I needed her to add that part. As if I couldn't feel the anger directed at me from all the girls. As if I could find an explanation that would solve this problem and put me back in everyone's good books again.

"You know what?" I said, looking at everyone individually before finishing. "I quit." It felt like the only thing to do. I haven't talked to them since.

It was weird not going to practice anymore, especially since my entire high school life I'd practised before and after school three times a week. We'd spend hours going over the music that our coach chose for our routines, loading it onto our iPods and listening to the songs until we knew every single beat by heart. As squad members, we ate lunch together, planned many of our outfits together, and spent hours with each other outside of school practising. It was like having another family, or at least I'd always thought of it that way until everyone started turning on me.

It's not that I didn't want to compete and win like everyone else, it's just that it took up so much time in my life, between my job, homework, and dance ... I'd been carrying on with this insane schedule for so many years and I just wanted a break.

Everyone thinks that Dylan has taken me away from them. And in a way, he has. But it's not that simple. Dylan doesn't play by anybody's rules and I admire that. That's why it's so refreshing to spend time with him. I'm tired of having everything set out for me already. Tired of all of the expectations. For once I want to do something unexpected, something out of character for me. Something so crazy that no one will believe it.

"What the hell?" The car slows a bit and Dylan looks back and forth from the road to his dashboard.

"What?" I ask.

"Do you hear that?"

"Hear what?" I have no idea what he's talking about.

"That knocking sound?" I strain to hear what he's hearing. Then I hear it, a faint knocking coming from the front of the car.

"My check engine light is on, too," Dylan says.

"Is this bad?" I ask.

"I don't know," he admits. "The car is still driving fine."

"Okay," I say, trying to reassure him. "Then it's probably nothing. We'll just keep driving."

"Come on!" Dylan's voice gets louder.

"What?! What's going on?"

We keep driving, but Dylan looks very uneasy.

"This is not the time ..." he mutters under his breath. His jaw is clenched.

"Maybe it's nothing ..." I venture.

"Maybe you should keep quiet," Dylan says to me. His eyes have darkened. I look at him, surprised. "Last time I checked, you weren't an auto mechanic."

Ouch. Except rather than keep my mouth shut I tell him, "Last time I checked you weren't either."

He shakes his head. "Really? Really? That's where you want this to go?"

"I'm just saying ... the car seems to be driving fine."

"Thank you, car expert. Now that I know we're fine, I will carry on." Dylan's voice drips with sarcasm. "You always have to be a know-it-all, don't you Annika?"

My cheeks flare with embarrassment. I'm not trying to be a know-it-all. I know that I can come across that way sometimes, but I'm really, truly just trying to be supportive.

"I just don't want you to be worried," I offer.

"No, of course. It's not your car, so why would you be worried? Did it occur to you that if we break down we might not make it to the cabin?"

"Of course that occurred to me!" I say. "I'm just trying to look on the bright side."

"Ah yes, the bright side. Annika Dietty's perfect life, where nothing bad has ever happened, where she can go on living a perfect existence with her perfect family in her perfect home. I forgot — you have no idea what reality is really like."

Anger surges through me. "My life isn't perfect, Dylan."

He smirks and shakes his head. "Riiiggghhhttt ..." he says. Why is he being such a jerk? It's true; my life has been easier than his. My family is still intact, still healthy. My parents have a pretty good marriage from what I can tell. I've done well in school, have had a pretty good job. I know that Dylan didn't really care for school and barely finished. He's had many different jobs and they don't usually work out. He finds himself in difficult situations all the time — more than anyone I know. It isn't fair for someone to go through so much. I suppose it would look like I've led a charmed life.

I decide to keep quiet and snuggle into the blanket. I watch the side of Dylan's face as he drives. He continues staring down at the dashboard and at the hood of the car. He knows something's up.

DYLAN

Before the engine started knocking, I'd been thinking of all the ways I could propose to Annika. I already know I'm going to marry her. I can't let someone like her get away. She's everything I've ever wanted — and so we might as well make it official. Yeah, we're young, but when you know, you know, right?

I imagined chartering a plane — one of those small ones. We'd go on a tour of the prairies, taking in the amazing scenery. Actually, no, I'd arrange for us to go skydiving. That was it. We'd jump out of a plane, holding hands, a literal plunge into our future. I'd have the people waiting below unroll a banner asking her to marry me. She'd see it as we head back to the refuge of the ground, and we'd land and she'd wrap her arms around me and shout, "Yes! A thousand times, yes!"

Or I could take her to Mexico or someplace warm and tropical. We could go scuba diving and I'd have a treasure box hidden on the bottom of the ocean. It'd have her name on it, and she'd open it, and see a gleaming diamond ring. And she'd know what it meant.

Or we could swim with dolphins and I could arrange something with the trainer. Perhaps a dolphin could bring her the ring, wrapped in some kind of package. She'd reach for the package, and lo and behold, the ring would be inside.

Then I thought maybe I should just surprise her with a full wedding. I could book a minister, buy her a dress, and decorate an area in her favourite colours, blue and white. We could get married right on the lot at the lake!

I'd arrange for a famous chef to have a meal waiting for us on a beautifully set table. I'd have Ed Sheeran playing for us as we have our first dance. Maybe I could hire a professional musician to come and play for us.

Would I invite family and friends? I didn't know. What if someone tried to stop the wedding? What if they talked Annika out of it? What if Annika decided that I wasn't the person for her after all? I'd have to plan something that showed her that I would do anything for her. I wanted her to feel like the most special woman in the world.

She's leaning against the car window, her eyes half closed like she'd like to sleep but doesn't want to miss anything either. Even though I'm pissed at her, I can't help noticing how angelic she looks, and I have to fight the urge to stare at her instead of the road. Then another coughing fit comes, this one intense and relentless. It's an awful sound, and I can tell it's taking the wind right out of her. She has to get some sleep. The sooner we get to the cabin, the better.

I think I'll make an excellent husband. I can't wait to be married, to start a family. I want to do it right. A one-time deal. My own parents never got it right. They argued more and more over the years. Mostly about me. I'm a hot topic among many, it seems. My own parents don't get me or support me in the ways that parents should. I'm never good enough. It does things to a person, this feeling of being discarded. Parents are supposed to be there for their children no matter what. They're not supposed to give up on them. That's what love is. Anni won't give up on me. She loves me.

The knocking sound in the engine is making me crazy. It's not very loud, but it's enough for me to know that something is wrong.

So now all I can think is *this can't be freakin' happening*. There's no way that we could finally be on the road, off to start our lives together only to have it all end with my stupid-ass car breaking down.

Despite Annika's naïve belief that everything will be fine, I know it won't. I spent all of my money buying the last of our supplies and getting us here in the first place. I don't have money for repairs or places to stay. This damn car has to get us there or else we're screwed.

I should've known this would happen. Nothing ever comes easy for me. I've been challenged my whole life, getting through things myself because I couldn't rely on anyone else. Because I'm a strong guy, who has experienced more than anyone can imagine.

My life is a series of bullshit, always threatening to put me under. Like when my friends Jake and Kyle ratted me out for sleeping in the boys' locker room at school. My parents had kicked me out. Just like that, they put me out on the street. What was I supposed to do? I had nowhere to go and it was winter. I decided that if I stayed in the school and hid out in different rooms, out of sight from the night caretakers, I could curl up in a change stall and sleep at night. It was genius — until Jake and Kyle went to the guidance counsellor and told her that I was sleeping there. She called my parents, who acted like they were happy to have me return home, as if they hadn't kicked me out in the first place.

Jake and Kyle tried to pass it off like they were trying to help me, like they were worried about me. But true friends don't rat each other out. That's like the first rule of friendship.

My parents forced me to get a job, but I had a hard time finding one. I didn't have a great-looking resume, all of those short-lived jobs. I tried to explain my bad luck to people who interviewed me, but no one wanted to give me a chance. Then my uncle offered me a job. I was supposed to be super grateful to him, but he acted like a drill sergeant and couldn't appreciate good work when he saw it. I'm used to people not recognizing my skills.

I know this is bad. I can feel it. Knocking sounds coming from the engine are practically sudden death. We're toast. Stranded-on-the-side-of-the-highway toast. Do we have any hope of making it all the way to the lake?

I could see the hurt in Annika's eyes when I snapped at her about it. That's the problem with Annika. She's lived this magically charmed life, so if you dare say something that she doesn't like, she acts as if she's just been horribly victimized. She's pretty sensitive.

All she knows is puppies and butterflies and all things gentle and good. She really has no concept of the way the world really works, and how it can chew you up and spit you out faster than you can imagine.

It's tough breaking the news to someone. The sooner she knows the better.

9:00 A.M.

ANNIKA

We stop at the convenience store and gas station on the side of the highway at the town of Shellbrook. Dylan fills the car up with gas and I head inside to go to the washroom. I have to wait in line, so I watch Dylan through the windows. He's chatting with another driver as they pump their gas. He says something that sends the other driver into hysterics. I smile. That's Dylan.

I watch them continue their conversation and then Dylan replaces the pump, waving goodbye to the man. Dylan walks in to the convenience store and kisses me on the forehead before going to pay.

"We should get some food," he says. I nod, and then it's my turn to use the washroom.

When I get in there it's grimy and smelly and I'm almost afraid to sit down. I go as quickly as I can and then wash my hands in record time, noting that there is no paper towel to dry my hands. I rub my hands on my thighs and then try to turn the doorknob with one finger.

"What's with that look?" Dylan says, smirking.

"It's gross in there," I say.

"What do you want?" We look around at the racks of chips and chocolate bars. There is even a basket with pastries wrapped in cellophane and fresh fruit.

I decide on a bag of chips and a Sprite, and Dylan buys chocolate. We walk up to the guy working the cash register, who is about our age.

"Your car the black hatchback?" he asks.

"Yup," Dylan says without even looking at him.

The cashier is tall and rod-thin. Acne peppers his cheeks and chin, but he has kind eyes and he's smiling.

"$32.50," he says.

Dylan opens his wallet and practically tosses two twenty-dollar bills at him. One of the bills tumbles off the counter and flutters to the ground in front of me. I look at Dylan, who is tapping his fingers impatiently on the counter, and he does not look impressed. I squat down to get the money and hand it back to the cashier, who thanks me and is still smiling but looks a bit puzzled by Dylan's mood.

"Here is your change," he says, handing back a bill and some coins. Dylan snatches it from him, turns on his heels, and heads for the car. The door to the store closes automatically and it nearly slams in my face as I follow Dylan.

"Thanks for getting the door …" I mutter sarcastically, but Dylan doesn't hear me. Instead he gets in the car, starts the ignition, and revs the engine.

I step into the car and fasten my seatbelt. Dylan pulls away from the gas station abruptly, his jaw clenched again. I decide to keep my mouth shut instead of ask him what's wrong. I glance out the window as we head back onto the highway, our speed picking up to match the other vehicles.

"Do you want to tell me what that was all about?" Dylan asks.

"What?"

"As if you don't know what I'm talking about," Dylan spits. I am genuinely perplexed. I have no idea what he's referring to. I mean, I thought Dylan was a bit rude to the clerk, but that's about it. I look at Dylan. He's shaking his head and smirking, but not in a nice way.

"The way you were flirting?"

"WHAT?!" I shriek. "Flirting? I didn't say a word to him!" Where in the world is he getting this? I picked up the money that fell and smiled at him, hoping to make up for Dylan's sour attitude. Period.

"I saw the way you guys were looking at each other. Here's something: maybe you shouldn't give some guy googly eyes when your boyfriend's around." My eyes must be bugging out of my head I'm so shocked. "Makes me wonder what you do when I'm not there."

"Dylan, please," I say, incredulous.

"Remember where your loyalties lie, Annika." He won't even glance at me now as I stare at him. He keeps his eyes fixed on the road ahead and ignores me. I'm so shocked I turn to look out the window again. The air feels like it's been sucked out of the car, along with any excitement we started out with. It's muggy and tense now, and I want to roll down my window to gulp some of the air and clear the negativity out but I know Dylan will just get more upset. I curl into myself and wrap my arms around my knees. Dylan looks over. He seems concerned about my bare feet on his seat but I don't care. I love having my feet bare and he'll just have to get used to it.

How could Dylan question how I feel about him? I've never once looked at another guy in that way. I've always supported him, tried to make him feel special and loved. In fact, I've dropped a lot of things and people to spend more time with him. Dylan hasn't had the supportive family life that I've had. I know how desperately he wants to be loved and cared for, and I've always tried my best to give that to him.

It's not the first time he's mistaken my intentions with someone. Paul, my neighbour, has been one of my closest friends since his family moved in next door fifteen years ago. We've literally been friends since we were potty training, and the first summer we met our moms would put us in one of those inflatable kiddie pools with our sun hats and our little water toys to entertain ourselves while the two of them visited. Paul is more like a brother to me than a friend, and we've always been really close even though we go to different schools, but he's never been a love interest. The two of them wanted to meet each other to find out about who I'd been gushing over for so long, but when they met, it didn't go over how I expected at all.

Paul had put his hand out for Dylan to shake, and as soon as their hands met, Dylan's mood seemed to change.

"Nice to meet you," Paul told him cheerfully. "Glad to meet the guy that Anni's been spending all her time with." He seemed genuinely happy for me and not at all jealous that we weren't spending as much time together anymore. He had a girlfriend himself, Kaitlin, and they'd been dating for months. Kaitlin and I liked each other. She didn't feel threatened by me, at least not that I knew of. She just seemed to accept that Paul and I were childhood friends first and foremost. Somehow Dylan thought that Paul was jealous, though, and he immediately gave him a solid stare.

"We should get together sometime, the four of us. Maybe go to a movie or something," Paul offered. Dylan clenched his jaw.

"Wouldn't you like that," he muttered.

"Excuse me?" Paul countered. He knitted his eyebrows together in confusion.

"Never mind!" I said cheerily as though it was all just a big joke. I would've liked to have gone on a double date with Paul and Kaitlin — they are a lot of fun to hang out with. But I knew Dylan would think that Paul had some ulterior motive, which couldn't be more ridiculous.

"We should go," I said. Dylan headed straight for the car without saying goodbye. I stood there awkwardly, being overly smiley.

"See you later! Have a great night!" I chirped to Kaitlin and Paul before joining Dylan at the car.

"Bye guys! Nice meeting you!" Kaitlin called out. Dylan didn't even acknowledge her. He sat looking straight out the windshield. I was embarrassed by his behaviour, especially when my eyes caught Paul's right before we drove off. It was unmistakable. His eyes held worry in them, and they were practically boring into my soul. I'd known him too long to think it was anything else. I'd talk to both of them, smooth things over. Assure both of them that everything was all right and that there was nothing to worry about. It was not how I envisioned their first meeting. Maybe all they'd need was some time and then we could all hang out together.

"What's the point of Paul keeping Kaitlin around?" Dylan asked.

"What do you mean?"

"Well, he says she's his girlfriend but it looks like he only has eyes for you."

"What?! That's ridiculous. He's crazy about Kaitlin. They've been together for months now. I don't know how many times I have to say this but me and Paul are just friends."

Later that night, after Dylan dropped me off, Paul was sitting on his front step. The boys didn't wave to each other or acknowledge one another.

"Hey, how was your day?" I asked him, sliding in beside him on the step.

"It was good. We went to see the new Avengers movie."

"Cool," I said. But there was this awkward silence hanging between us. Like Paul had a lot to say but wasn't saying it. I fiddled with my shoelace and tried to ignore my thoughts. Things between Paul and me had always been easy, comfortable. This feeling was new and it sucked.

"So, Dylan …" Paul finally said.

I waited for a "he seems like a nice guy" or a "we should hang out sometime," but nothing came. Nothing.

"He's a really great guy once you get to know him," I assured Paul. He smirked.

"Yeah, basically accusing me of wanting you right in front of my girlfriend. First impression: he's charming."

"He's just weirded out by our friendship — how close we are."

"That's crap, Anni. Kaitlin never had a problem handling it. Because we're friends. That's it."

"You have to admit, there are people who'd have a hard time with us. I mean, we can practically finish each other's sentences. And our families are just that, family. I think it'd be normal for someone to need time to adjust to that and not feel threatened by it."

"I think you're with the wrong dude, then," Paul countered.

"He'll come around."

"He shouldn't have to!" Paul shook his head. "Just be careful, Anni."

Why can't guys and girls be friends? Even my girlfriends thought our relationship was too close to be just friendship. Why does everyone assume that we're actually in love with each other? I've seen Paul at his worst — the time he broke his arm falling from the tree fort at his grandma's and he cried for six hours straight, his bout with Rotavirus last year when he lost five pounds just from vomiting so much. I felt so bad I hung out in the doorway watching his mother stroke his forehead while they sat on the bathroom floor. He even got admitted to the hospital and was put on an IV because of dehydration. I'd stayed with him the whole time. I'd even been the one to help shield him when he pooped his pants in grade one. I'd walked directly behind him until he got to the washroom and then I ran to tell the teacher so that she could call his mom. I never told a soul. No one.

Paul has also been privy to some of my most embarrassing moments, like when my mom told his mom that I still wet the bed even though I was eight. (Thankfully I'd grow out of it.) Or the day I got my first period. We were out riding our bikes near the lake (a man-made pond really, but they insist on building newer communities around "lakes" to make them sound much more prestigious). I stood up to pedal up the hilly path that surrounded the water when Paul yelled, "Ew!!!"

"What?" I looked around on the grass and the cement to see what he was talking about. I expected a dead bird or rotting food or something but the path looked clear.

"You're bleeding!" His face had this look of disgust.

"What?! Where?" I'd never dreamed I'd be bleeding from there.

"I think you got your you-know-what ..." Paul said and then he started laughing uncontrollably. I started to cry. Immediately I could tell Paul felt bad. He got off of his bike and draped an arm around my shoulder.

"Sorry, Anni. I didn't mean to laugh. It's okay, Anni. Let's go home." I was so embarrassed, even though it was Paul. I didn't want him to see this. "I won't tell anyone. Promise," Paul said. And he didn't.

He has always called me the sister he's never had. He's an only child. His parents always wanted more children, but I know they tried for years without any success. Instead our families kind of melded together. Maybe in a storybook world, Paul and I hooking up would be the happily-ever-after, the perfect story that our parents could tell for years to come. But in the real world we are just friends.

"He'll come around," I repeated to Paul that day with Dylan. But even I wasn't sure. After that, I started seeing Paul less — he had plans with Kaitlin a lot of the time and I was with Dylan when I wasn't working, and we sure weren't getting together as couples. Dylan liked us to keep to ourselves. I was cool with that — I'd lost other friends to their boyfriends. They'd meet a guy and suddenly have no time left for me anymore. I hadn't understood it before, but now that I had Dylan in my life, it made sense. We wanted to spend all of our time together.

"You are the only one for me, babe," I tell him, rubbing his arm. Dylan's jaw is set and he keeps looking straight ahead at the road, but I can tell he's softening a bit. "I adore you and only you."

Dylan's hand settles on my leg and I know we're good again.

DYLAN

All I can think while I'm pumping gas is how much I hope that the car will start again. We only have about another hour to go. Maybe we can still make it. My stomach churns with anxiety.

A souped-up shiny black pick-up truck pulls up to the pump next to me. I practically salivate. It's a Dodge Ram Power Wagon 4x4 with a 6.4-litre HEMI V8. It's the truck of my dreams. The first thing I'd buy if I won the lottery or something. I imagine myself behind the wheel of that, instead of my limping piece of crap. I will have that truck someday, and I'll know I've finally made it.

A middle-aged man steps out of the truck. He's wearing paint-splattered coveralls and steel-toed boots. A man who knows a hard day of work and has earned everything he has, I think to myself.

"Nice truck," I nod to him.

"Thanks," he says, smiling.

I notice the plywood in the box of the truck. We're like two kindred spirits.

"Whatcha working on?" I ask.

"A house up on Second Street," he replies. "A real wreck. We've gutted to stud."

"Those are always fun," I smile. "I just finished the new CIBC on Ritter in Saskatoon."

"That's a big project," he says. "I'm renovating for my daughter and her kids. A family of hoarders lived there before. There was stuff to the ceiling in some rooms. Couldn't even walk in there."

"Gross." I shake my head. "I'm sure there were a lot of surprises in there!"

"Mice, mould, bugs, even feces," he says wryly.

"Hope you got it for a song," I say, and he throws back his head with a hearty laugh.

"Yeah, they should have paid me to take the house, I think."

"Well, good luck with everything," I say.

"Thanks. Take care!" he calls out to me.

I step into the gas station. The bells on the front door jangle and startle me. I'm so worried that the car won't start again and we'll be stranded that I feel beads of sweat forming on my forehead. My heart is starting to pound, like a steady drum getting stronger and stronger. I can't let Annika down, I can't get us this far and then have us stuck on the side of the road. She'll think we won't be okay on our own, that I can't handle things, and she'll want to go back home. She'll realize I'm broke and that there is no other plan. She'll wonder what the heck she's doing with me and she'll cut out as soon as she can.

She lights up when I get to her and my anxiety quells a bit. Her smile is like a warm blanket, enveloping me in joy. She is perfection. I wait for her while she goes to the washroom. When she gets out, she has this weird look on her face. I try to stay cool, assure myself that it has nothing to do with me. She tells me the bathroom was gross — but I can't help but sense that maybe she's worried about everything and that she thinks I'm a loser for having such a crappy car.

We each choose some food for the road, and all I can think about is the fact that we might not be going anywhere and how could this be happening? Annika must think I'm such a tool. There's no reason for a girl like her to be with a guy like me and the first chance she gets, she's going to bolt. I knew she couldn't possibly love someone like me.

We walk up to the cashier and I hand him enough money to cover the tab. My hands are starting to shake and my heart is hammering in my chest again. A steady rhythm that seems to echo louder in my ears. I want to shut my eyes and tune it all out. Why won't this cashier give me my change already? Then I see Annika reaching down for something on the floor and I watch as the cashier smiles and thanks her. She is smiling back at him too, and my heart lurches into my throat. It's happening. She's into him, and realizing that I'm no good for her. If that car doesn't start, she'll abandon me right here and run off with this guy — who clearly has a job and probably a perfectly running vehicle around the back.

I'm sweating and shaking. I've got to get back out to the car. I dart for the car and hop in quickly, desperate to find out if our fate's been sealed. I place the key in the ignition, my hands a bit unsteady, and to my surprise, the car turns over easily. Relief floods over me.

Please get us out of here, I bargain. *I'll do anything. Anything if we can just make it up to the cabin.*

I step on the gas with some force and the tires squeal as we leave the station. I can still hear the knocking sound, but it isn't any louder, so I'll drive for as long as I can. I think back to what happened in the gas station. Although I'm relieved about the car, my anxiety's been replaced with the sick feeling that Annika will leave.

I picture her and the cashier smiling at each other, their hands touching when she passes him the money, and my skin grows warm and my heart gets to hammering again. Why does she have to flash her smile at other guys? Doesn't she know that she's flirting with them? And why is she flirting with them when she's supposed to be with me?

I can't help but feel like if there's any sign of trouble, my girl, who supposedly loves me, will jump ship at the first opportunity. I better let her know that I've caught everything and that if she thinks that she can sneak around behind my back, it's not happening.

I try to talk to her about it, but she acts like she has no idea what I'm talking about. She looks at me pleadingly, with her big doe eyes, but I'm not buying it.

"You are the only one for me, babe," she says, rubbing my arm. "I adore you and only you."

The touch of her hand on my arm sends goosebumps up my body. Instantly, I feel her touch and I want to wrap myself in her arms instead of driving this car. I feel my heart rate lower, and I start to relax. I reach over and rest my hand on her leg.

She said it herself. I'm the only one for her. My girl's not going anywhere.

10:00 A.M.

ANNIKA

We are standing on the side of the road. Dylan is pacing and grabbing his hair with his fists. He's kicked the tires and the passenger's side door multiple times, and now there is a visible dent in the side of the car. Dylan thinks the engine has died, and there is no easy way for us to get it fixed.

"It's okay, Dylan," I try to reassure him. "We'll find a way."

I'm reluctant to offer more, in case he chews my head off like last time, but he's acting like this is the end of the world. It's not. We can get beyond this.

There isn't much traffic for a weekday morning on this stretch of highway. The car's hazard lights flash rhythmically.

"Should we call a tow truck?" I offer. That's what my parents would do. They have CAA and all they have to do is call the number on the card. Dylan isn't a member, but it seems logical that we should probably get the car towed to the nearest town somehow.

Dylan shakes his head. "It'll cost us a fortune," he says.

I don't really see how we have a choice. We can't just leave the car here with all of our stuff.

We hear the sound of a vehicle approaching, and sure enough a truck is headed our way.

The navy blue crew cab slows as it approaches.

"Car trouble?" the man asks. He's probably in his seventies. He's wearing a worn ball cap and a plaid button-up shirt, and he has white stubble blanketing his cheeks.

"Yeah, I think the engine's toast," Dylan admits. "Was driving just fine until we heard a ticking a ways back."

"A ticking? Yeah, that's never a good sound," the man agrees. "Can I give you two a lift? Where you headed?" He's looking at all of the gear we have stuffed in the hatchback.

"Delaronde. You know how it is. Worked my tail off all summer. Time for a vacation," Dylan says.

"No better place than the lake," the man smiles. "We could throw all of your stuff into the back of the truck and I'll take you up there."

"We'd really appreciate that, sir," Dylan says. "I'll call my dad to come and get the car."

"Well, let's get that stuff loaded in here and I'll get you back on your way."

I feel instant relief. We'll still get to the cabin and we can take all of our things with us. For a while there, I was scared that Dylan might suggest we walk the rest of the way. We're pretty close by car but it would be a long walk, especially with all our gear.

We each take turns grabbing things out of the car. It's amazing how much Dylan managed to fit. Dylan and the man hoist up the cooler, which is the last item, and the next thing I know I'm buckling my seatbelt in the back seat of a stranger's truck. If I should be nervous, I'm not. This man, whose name turns out to be George, is kind and eager to assist us. His truck is very clean, and he whistles easily as he drives, telling us about his farmland not too far from Delaronde where his family has been going for three generations now.

Dylan and he chat easily, and when they get talking about fishing, I phase out and stare out the window. The spruce trees here are gorgeous, their dark green juxtaposed against the oranges, yellows, and reds of the other trees and shrubs. The leaves from the rest of the trees have mostly fallen, and they look bright and beautiful lying on the green of the grass.

Clouds are rolling in, and the sun's rays peek out here and there. I think of how it won't be long before the really cold weather sets in and how different it will be to spend winter somewhere like this. We pass several road signs that warn of possible wildlife, and then two sandy-coloured deer dart across the road in front of us. I marvel at their speed and grace.

I think of Monday. It will be weird not to be in class. I wonder what my friends will say when they realize I'm not there. Will they miss me? Cheerleading has been going strong right from the start because of football season. I've always enjoyed the return to school in the fall. I love the feeling of a new start: the anticipation of what classes you'll be in, who your teachers will be, and who'll be in your class. I love opening blank notebooks and textbooks and the smell of freshly sharpened pencils.

Mom bought me school supplies weeks ago. I couldn't tell her that they wouldn't get much use. She brought them home knowing how much I enjoy getting new school supplies year after year, so I had no choice but to feign excitement.

I wonder what my parents are doing now. Saturday mornings are pretty lax in our house. They must be awake. They're probably lounging in the living room in their robes and slippers, sipping coffee and flipping through the newspaper, oblivious to the fact that I'm gone.

I wonder how long it will take them to notice. They'll assume I am sleeping in. And when they pop in later in the day and see that I'm not there, they might assume I went for a run or to a friend's house. I don't imagine they'll check in for a while. But they will check in. They like to know where I am at all times practically. They aren't big fans of letting me hang out in public places for hours at a time like a lot of my friends do. They're always so scared that something's going to happen to me. I wish they'd have more faith in me and my ability to take care of myself. I mean, I'm a good kid. I wish they'd learn to trust me more.

I still haven't figured out what I'll do and how I'll break it to them when they do discover that I'm not at home. I need to buy as much time as I can, and somehow reassure them that all is fine. I'll tell them that they are welcome to come and visit us, if and only if they can accept that Dylan and I are staying together.

The truck slows to turn down a well-treed road, and I realize that there are cabins tucked in among the trees. Many are newer, large two-storey cabins. They are a lot fancier than I expected.

As if reading my mind, George pipes up. "No one seems to know what a cabin is anymore. These days, they're building these big mansions instead. My grandfather would roll over in his grave if he saw these monstrosities."

"We're down the next lane," Dylan instructs.

Many of the lots are so dense with trees that it makes it hard to see the cabins. This excites me, this feeling of being tucked away in the woods. It's not at all what I expected.

"Right here," Dylan says. We stop in front of a one-and-a-half-storey log cabin. It's an older place, definitely different from the newer builds we first saw when we drove in.

It's tidy and well-kept, especially for having sat vacant for so long. There are welcome signs tacked to the railing of the wraparound deck, and rock-lined flower beds that have ceramic ornaments like frogs and squirrels amid the yellow wildflowers that grow there. I immediately fall in love with the place.

George steps out and opens the truck's hatch.

"You need any help getting settled?" George asks.

"I think you've helped us enough," Dylan says. "We'll just unload right here and Annika and I can do the rest. I really appreciate what you've done for us."

Dylan pulls out a ten dollar bill and hands it to George.

"Oh, heavens, no." George shakes his head. "I don't want your money. Happy to help. Have a good vacation. Safe travels home."

Safe travels home…. Little does he know, *this* is home now.

DYLAN

Should've known that piece of metal wouldn't get me all the way. It was just my luck, as always, that everything would fall apart as soon as something good was about to happen to me. Like the universe conspires to keep me down just when I'm on my way to happiness.

Then this man named George comes along, asking if he can help us get to where we need to go. It's nice of him, but I wish we could have figured things out on our own. I wasn't crazy about this guy dropping us off, but Annika looked so relieved, I didn't really have a choice.

Annika is talking a mile a minute now as we stand in the driveway of the cabin. My own heart is thumping in my chest. We're drawing too much attention with our gear on the side of the road and Annika chattering away. I've got to get us in this place before anyone comes around.

"Stay here with our stuff," I tell her. It's not as though anyone is going to steal it, but I want her to stay put. She's looking around in wonder, absorbing the landscape around her. I make my way toward the back of the cabin.

There are sticks in the windows so that they can't be slid open. The door to the cabin is on the side. When I approach it, Annika is no longer in view. Thank goodness. The door is locked, of course. I rattle the doorknob, and the door feels a bit loose and light, like it wouldn't take much to get it open … but if I break the doorknob, how will we close it properly?

I reach into my pocket and pull out my trusty red Swiss Army knife. This thing has helped me out more times than I can count. I take out the smallest knife and feed it into the door lock, hoping it'll cause the lock to click open. Beads of sweat are forming on my forehead. This has to work quickly, otherwise Annika will wonder where I am and come looking for me. Knowing how excited she is, I'm surprised she's still standing at the road, that she didn't just follow me here.

The lock clicks, and, sure enough, the door pops open when I turn the knob. Thank god. I swing the door open. It smells a bit musty, as though it's been closed up for a few weeks already, which it most likely has. The lights don't come on, so I take a quick look around for the breaker panel before calling for Annika.

"Your home awaits, my love!" I call out from the deck. Little does she know my armpits are soaked; I can even feel the sweat trickling down my back and chest. Anni laughs. I run toward her to so that we can carry our things in. When she enters the cabin, she gushes.

"This is awesome," she says. "I just love it!" The walls are covered in pine tongue-and-groove siding, and framed prints of nature and lake scenery are tacked on the walls. It isn't big, but it's cozy and clean. The fridge is propped open with a broom. I spot the woodstove in the corner.

"I'll get a fire going right away, Anni. It'll warm up fast."

Annika is practically running from room to room, taking it all in. There are two small bedrooms upstairs; otherwise everything is on the main floor.

"We're home!" Annika is elated. She's spinning in a circle with her arms outstretched.

"We're home, babe." My voice is husky and full. I catch her arm and pull her into me for a long kiss. We stand there entwined, and one kiss becomes many. My whole body tingles with desire and I want to take her to the bedroom right now. We're finally alone. I can't believe we've done it. We're here. With our things. We're staying.

"I'm so happy," Annika whispers. "Should we get unpacked?"

I reluctantly let her go. She's probably right. After we get settled, there will be plenty of time for us.

She empties the cooler while I take our bags up to our bedroom. I can hear her coughing downstairs. Then she stops and quiet blooms. I'm drinking this place in myself. Flashbacks of all kinds enter my mind.

The wooden bench on the landing — the first thing I ever built with my hands. Dad had given me a hammer and nails and some scrap wood. "Keep busy," he'd said. So I took a pencil and drew a chicken-scratch design of the bench so that I could follow a plan of some sort. I'd stayed busy all right — I worked on that thing for about six hours straight. I didn't even stop to eat supper or the cookies and can of pop my mom brought out for me. I had a laser-like focus, and I was determined to get that thing built before sundown.

It's funny that it took me so long to build the darn thing, considering how Mickey Mouse it looks to me now. I guess everyone's gotta start somewhere. That's when I first discovered that I liked building things, which led to taking houses that had seen better days and making them look great again. There's something hopeful about breathing new life into what others would consider long gone. I can't believe that bench is still here.

I glance down from the upstairs railing overlooking the living room below. I remember all of the fires in that old wood stove. Many times Dad and I would rub our stiff, icy hands near the radiating heat after brisk morning fishing trips. We even cooked hotdogs and marshmallows over the flames when the doors were open.

I throw our bags on the bed in one of the bedrooms. It's a small room, but there is light streaming in the window in shimmery slivers as it beams through the forest trees. It looks inviting and peaceful. There's a thick patchwork quilt on the bed and a three-drawer antique dresser in the room, the walls covered in the same tongue-and-groove pine found throughout the rest of the cabin. Dad had tacked that up himself, along with a couple of my uncles. I wasn't around for it — things weren't so hot between us at that time. Dad was trying to keep me close — reined in and under his thumb — and I wanted no part of it. I was going to do my own thing whether he liked it or not. By that point, I was done listening to what he had to say.

I rummage through the side pocket of my tote bag. My fingers land on the soft velvet box. It's not the engagement ring I'm going to give her someday, but it's something to show her how serious I am. I'm in this for the long haul.

"Dylan, are you coming back down here?" Annika calls out.

Smiling, I run down the stairs to her and pick her up before she even knows I'm behind her.

"Ahh!" she shrieks, but she's laughing as I twirl her around, my arms wrapped around her waist. I kiss the back of her head, and her fruit-scented hair tickles my nose.

I hold the box out in front of her.

"What?!" She spins toward me.

"Open it."

She takes the box gingerly from me and opens it carefully. I watch as her eyes light up at the delicate gold ring. There's a pretty diamond set into the top of it.

"Dylan!" She pulls it out of the box and slides it on. I smile when she chooses her ring finger. That's exactly where I wanted it to go.

"It's a promise ring," I tell her. "I know it's not much … but I promise to love you forever."

Annika is beaming. Tears spring from her eyes and I wipe them gently with my thumbs. We hold each other close. Her body pressed against mine is enough to drive me wild. Annika coughs again, and nestles into my neck.

"Thank you, Dyl. I love it. I love you."

"Someday it'll be the real thing," I assure her. "You want to go upstairs and lie down?"

There's nothing I'd like more than for us to head up to the bed together. My hands travel over her shoulders, and through her bra straps. The straps slide down her arms. I lean down to kiss her collarbone. Annika smiles, but wiggles away from me. She shakes her head.

"I think I'd like some fresh air," she says. "It might make me feel better."

I feel a pang of disappointment but I know she's sick, and we'll have lots of time to be together.

"We could walk out to the beach. I'll show you what I've been talking about."

"Okay," she agrees.

"Maybe I'll even catch us a fish for supper while we're there," I offer. I'm so pumped to start our lives here together. It's going to be everything I've dreamed of.

It's time to blow this cookie joint. I'm going to take my girl fishing. Finally.

11:00 A.M.

ANNIKA

This place is amazing. It's a bit smaller than I expected, but it's perfect for the two of us. I'm looking forward to all of the adventures that await us. Dylan isn't as excited as I thought he'd be. He's acting a little weird. I mean, he picked me up and twirled me around, and he keeps kissing me, but he also seems a bit edgy and distracted.

Ever since we pulled up and got settled, he's been a bit jumpy and reactive. At first I thought it was because he was nervous to give me this gorgeous ring that I'm wearing, but I can't help but feel like there's more. I want to ask him what's wrong, but I think better of it. This is all new, and we did leave our families to come here without them knowing, so he's probably processing all of that.

Speaking of our families, my phone has been dinging with texts non-stop. A few from friends asking if I'll be at Ryan Lewis's party tonight, and one from a co-worker asking if I'll take a shift for her. She's just coming back after being on maternity leave for a year, so she must not know that I no longer work there. But mostly they are from my mom.

Where are you? 10:31 a.m.

Are you feeling better? 10:52 a.m.

Are you out for a run? 10:53 a.m.

Let me know where you are… 11:05 a.m.

Do you want to go to the mall with me later? 11:07 a.m.

Anni, why haven't I heard from you? Answer me please!!! 11:08 a.m.

And one missed call, also at 11:08. My mom has always been such a worrier. In the forty-five minutes she hasn't heard from me, she's probably decided that I've been horribly injured, in a car wrapped around a tree somewhere remote, where there is no hope of rescuing me. Or maybe she's envisioning me on a morning run, some creep keeping pace not too far from me, waiting for the opportune time to attack. As twisted as it sounds, she's probably already planning my funeral.

I don't know what to say. At least not yet. How do I tell them that I'm gone for good? How will I break the news to them? I have to just keep them at bay as long as I can.

I'm fine. I'll call you in a bit. 11:12 am

I switch my phone to vibrate and stuff it in my pocket.

Dylan calls for me. I pop a couple of Tylenol into my mouth and swallow them down before I head downstairs to join him. Together we pick up the fishing gear that he's lined up on the deck. We make our way down the driveway to the main road.

Dylan reaches for me. We juggle the fishing supplies so that we can hold hands while we walk. I look down several times to see the small diamond in my ring glisten when my hand moves. Wearing this ring thrills me. It makes me believe in the promise of the future. I'm right where I'm supposed to be. With Dylan.

The air smells heavy and sweet. There doesn't seem to be another soul around. It's quiet and peaceful. Most of the other cabins are well hidden by forest; the only hint of their existence are the gravel approaches between the tree clearings. I try to catch glimpses of the cabins in each lot as we walk by.

"Maybe one day we can buy our own cabin," I suggest. Dylan smiles and squeezes my hand.

I see half of the front of a cute one-storey cabin as we walk by. It has a wraparound porch that I can imagine stringing Christmas lights from in the winter and pretty coloured lanterns in the summer.

"Ooh, I love that one!" I point, but Dylan shakes his head.

"Or we could build our own," he winks. I know how much he'd love to build our dream home on a piece of land here.

"Definitely build our own!" I agree. My mind flashes to older versions of us in front of a sprawling log home tucked into the trees. It has a welcome sign at the driveway. There are even dark-haired mini versions of Dylan tearing through the yard on their little bikes.

It's amazing how someone can imagine their whole life with another person when they are this young. I'm so lucky to have found the person I'll spend my life with.

Only a few minutes later, we come to a bend in the road, which leads us to what must be the beach. The water is rough and menacing, the waves batter the shore. As we approach the open sand, the wind picks up and whips our faces. I struggle a bit for air but the cool wind also soothes my fevered face.

There is an aging wooden dock that leads out about thirty feet from the shore. It creaks a bit when we stand on it but feels secure despite its worn boards. We walk to the end of it and Dylan sets down the tackle box and hands me a rod. I set down the net, the gloves, and the bag of snacks I've brought. I look at the rod dumbly, not having the first clue of how to bait the hook and set up the line for casting.

Dylan works quickly, his nimble fingers adept at knotting the fishing line. A shiny metal hook that looks like a little fish flashes in the sun. I try to follow what he's doing, but I can't keep up to with his fine movements. He looks up at me and smiles.

I see the sun dancing off of his dark hair and his eyes lit up and my heart skips a little. This is Dylan in his element. His enthusiasm is infectious, and although I've never really fished before, I want to love it. I want to learn everything about it so that we can do this together. I want to capture the joy and contentment in this moment and keep it forever.

He trades me rods so that he can get mine ready. I look out over the water, unable to see the other side of the lake. It's a big body of water. I see a hawk land on the top of a spruce tree just down from the beach. I'm looking forward to seeing wildlife on a regular basis. Once again, I'm struck by the fact that it feels like we have this whole place to ourselves.

I feel my phone buzz in my pocket. Do I dare take a look? My stomach knots. I know exactly who is texting me. Dylan is preoccupied with my fishing rod so I decide to take a peek.

Okay. Call me soon then. 11:34 a.m.

Ugh. If I don't call her right away, she'll call the police. I know it. Before the morning is up there will be an entire police force out looking for me if she has any say in the matter.

"Who's texting you?" Dylan asks.

"My mom," I say softly. I know he's not going to like this.

"Have you told her where you are?"

"No. I haven't said anything yet."

"You were right about her," Dylan smirks. "She really doesn't let you have any space. I'm surprised she lets you out of the house at all."

"I'm sure she'd keep me inside if she could," I laugh. At the same time though, I feel a pang of guilt. I mean, usually I am just at a friend's house or out for a run. I'm usually only a few minutes away and doing something completely reasonable. Not moving across the province with my boyfriend to a remote area that no one will suspect.

"I better respond to her," I tell him. "Otherwise she'll probably call the police."

Dylan rolls his eyes.

But I can't do it. I can't tell them yet. I'll work up to it. For now I just want to enjoy this day with Dylan and celebrate our newfound freedom together. I'll make something up. If I tell her I'm at Tara's or Ali's house, she'll definitely call over there. This is my mom we're talking about. I have to think of someplace where she can't track me.

I'm spending the day with Elise. It's her birthday. I'll be home later. 11:36 a.m.

Elise??? 11:36 a.m.

My friend. You've met her. At the track meet, remember? 11:37 a.m.

I am not being totally honest here. My mom did meet an Elise at the track meet, but she goes to another school. Elise's parents were seated next to mine at the track meet and that's how we met. Our parents introduced us to each other as we joined them after the meet, both of us sweaty and panting from the last relay of the day. We really didn't know each other at all. Hopefully Mom doesn't question me further.

Okay. Text me later. 11:38 a.m.

I breathe a sigh of relief and shove my phone back into my pocket. They have no idea how to reach Elise and her family so I'm good there. I've bought myself some time before I really tell them what's going on.

DYLAN

I've got my arms wrapped around Annika, my hands over hers grasping the fishing rod. I've been showing her how to cast properly and she's finally getting the hang of it. At first I was getting frustrated … how hard is it to press a button, flick your wrist, and let go? But then I decide to take in the moment, namely having my arms wrapped around her like this.

She looks so beautiful, this side profile of her face and the way the wind is sending her hair flying behind her. I've caught a mouthful of it a few times but it's totally worth it. She seems to like fishing quite a bit. She keeps giggling every time she feels any kind of tension on her line. Thank god she likes fishing. I can't imagine a girl of mine not liking fishing. That's what we do out here.

Maybe I'll even get her into hunting. I know she turns her nose up at it now but I think she'll change her mind once we get out there and she experiences it for the first time. There's something about the thrill of the chase, the feeling of absolute mastery.

The wind seems to be picking up, though, and I think there may be a storm at some point, the way the darker clouds are moving in. I look at the tree line surrounding the lake and breathe deeply. I never tire of this smell — the fresh pine air that seems to soothe me like nothing else. The lake is quiet today; I can't hear any boats but the water is pretty rough, so I'm not too surprised.

The water slaps the sand in a rhythmic motion. White foam sprays all over the pebbles on the shore. It's a great time to catch a fish. If Annika learns how to do this properly, we might actually catch something and then we'll be eating fresh fish tonight. It'll be the perfect meal to start our life here together.

I hear Annika's phone buzzing again. It's probably her overprotective crazy mother who can't seem to last five minutes without having her daughter under her thumb. It's unhealthy how tight she hangs on. I picture ripping the phone out of her pocket and throwing it into the lake, its shiny pink case shimmering as it sinks. I can't tell you how much joy that would bring me.

"Are you ready to do this on your own now?" I ask. I set my fishing rod down to help her and I'd really like to get back to fishing so we can have that meal I've been dreaming about tonight.

"I don't think I've quite got it yet," Annika coos. She's smirking and resting her head on my shoulder. *Yeah*, I think. *Screw fishing*. Annika's practically batting her eyelashes at me, and she looks so happy. I'll stay right where I am. As the wind picks up, standing together keeps us both warmer. I place my hands on her hips and I feel her settle into me. I groan, feeling her pressed up against me, and she giggles.

"Are you sure you want to keep fishing? I can think of something else we could be doing right now," I whisper to her. She gives me a mischievous smile and then turns back to her rod.

"Oh my god! I think I've got something!" she shrieks. She's no longer leaning against me but is standing on her tiptoes on the dock, her eyes wide. She looks a little scared. Sure enough, her rod has formed a large bend.

"Calm down!" I tell her. "Just keep your rod steady. And keep reeling. Slow and steady …"

I put my arms around her again to help but she shakes me off this time. It stings a little. Why wouldn't she want my help?

"I want to do it myself," she says. She's practically

jumping all around the dock and she's going to lose him if she keeps this up.

"Settle down, Anni," I scold. "You're going to lose him."

"Let me do it!" she insists. I try to grab the rod to help steady it and Annika moves to the edge of the dock a few steps away from me.

"What are you doing?!" I yell. She's just taken away the tension on the rod by moving up a few feet. She's probably given that fish the perfect escape opportunity now.

"Let me do it!"

I try to bite my tongue and just let her reel the fish in, but she's doing everything wrong. She'll be lucky if there's even a fish on the end of the hook. If she'd just stop and listen to me … I shake my head. I watch her clumsily manage the rod as the line gets closer and she's barely keeping herself together, let alone the reeling of the fish.

"He's coming! He's coming!" she yells. Sure enough, a jackfish pops out of the water, tearing around trying to free himself. It is probably an eight- or nine-pound fish. Its long olive body continues to thrash, and the closer he gets to Annika, the more she freaks out.

"Oh my god, oh my god, oh my god!!!" she repeats over and over again. Her excitement has turned to fear. She looks like she might pass out. "He's huge! And he's all spotted!"

I reach for the net that's been resting at our feet but Annika is jumping around so much she kicks it into the water. I groan as I watch it bobbing beside the dock.

The fish's yellow spots glisten as the water drips off

of his body. He's a beauty and he'll be tasty tonight. He's dangling in mid-air so I grab the rod from Annika, who's more than happy to let it go now.

"On second thought, hold this…," I tell her. I hand the rod back to her. If she holds it steady, I can wriggle the hook from the fish's mouth and put him in the bucket.

"Ew," she shrieks as she watches the fish writhe. I'm trying to detach the fish from the hook but everything is moving from me.

"Hold still!" I yell.

"I am!"

"Not still enough!"

I manage to pry the hook from the inside of the fish's mouth and once Annika sees that he's free, she drops the rod and moves back.

"Pass me the bucket," I tell her. I take one of my hands off of the fish to grab the bucket and the next thing I know, my hands are empty and I hear a plop as the fish hits the water once again. He swims away before I can do anything.

Annika and I look at each other. She bursts out laughing. I am not impressed.

"I caught my first fish!" she smiles.

"Well, technically you didn't, otherwise we'd still have him." I can feel my blood pressure rising. "That was supposed to be our supper."

She looks at me strangely, as though it doesn't matter what we eat for supper. But she doesn't understand. We only have so much food right now. We can't go wasting it all on the first few days. I was depending on that fish to feed us.

"We'll get one," she shrugs, as though an abundance

of fish will magically materialize. Once again, Annika's perfect life is magnified. The world she lives in is one where everything always works out. You just have to have the right attitude and stay positive and all will be well. Except it won't. She just hasn't learned this yet.

"It would've been fine if you'd been calm like I told you," I point out.

"You're the one who let go of it!" she says.

"And why was that, Annika? Because you couldn't even hold a bucket up to him. It was a fish, not the freakin' Loch Ness Monster."

"I was just a little freaked out," she says, her voice getting smaller.

"Well, that's just great. You caused us to lose that fish. Now we're down a meal."

"I'll try again," she offers.

"No. I think we've had *all* the fishing we can handle for one day," I mutter. I get down on my knees and put my arm in the water to collect the fishing net. I gather the rest of the fishing gear and start back down the dock, leaving Annika there. I wait to hear her footsteps behind me, but it's quiet. She's probably pouting, thinking I'm too hard on her.

That's the problem. Her parents have been too soft. She's too coddled. I thought we were a good match but trying to console her and manage her feelings takes a lot of work. Leaving her at the dock is a good thing. Maybe she'll come to see that this was all her fault after all.

1:00 P.M.

ANNIKA

Dylan is melting butter in the frying pan and as it sizzles I realize how hungry I am. He has arranged cheese slices neatly between pieces of bread for grilled cheese. His jaw is set, his eyebrows are knitted together. He slaps the sandwiches down in the pan and puts the butter back into the fridge and then kicks the door shut. It closes with a loud thud.

I swallow. The air is thick and tense between us. I tried engaging him by being overly cheery once I got back to the cabin but he hasn't said a word to me since we were at the beach trying to fish. Surely he can't be that mad over a fish, can he? It's not like we'll never have an opportunity to fish again with us living here now.

Maybe he's mad that I didn't run after him trying to smooth things over, but I felt a little shocked by another one of his mood swings. It was only a fish. Instead I watched him trudge back to the cabin, his legs making large, purposeful strides.

I sat on the dock, taking in gulps of air as the wind whipped my hair across my face. It made me feel alive — evidence that I was there, in existence. Looking out over the vast body of water without another human in sight, I realized how small I actually felt. A tinge of loneliness crept over me, and I shivered in the wind. A new thought nagged at me. Was I small because of the landscape or was I small because of Dylan's words?

It wasn't the first time Dylan had what I thought was an overreaction to something. He tended to react in large ways to practically anything — good or bad. It was one of the things I first loved about him as I watched him play basketball. He took the game seriously, and he played hard every minute he was on the court. He had something special that most of the guys out there didn't have, and you could see it. It was passion. He played the game with pure passion etched on his face and in his every move. I admired that. Sure, I had things I loved about myself, too, but I'd never seen someone who put his heart and soul into something like that.

Dylan had been the lead scorer on our high school's basketball team since grade eleven when he joined the team. I don't know why he hadn't joined sooner given how good he was, but I didn't really know who he was until the day he first stepped out onto the court his junior year. I wasn't the only one who noticed him — the crowd went wild for this new kid.

Mr. Wilson, our senior basketball coach, was practically jumping out of his skin with excitement watching Dylan dominate the court. We laughed at how his eyes bulged out of his head and how he'd grab his hair and jump up and down whenever Dylan scored. It's not that we had a bad team before that, it's just that Dylan brought it to a new level. Coach Wilson knew it and so did the crowd.

I remember sitting in the bleachers, half-heartedly eating popcorn after the first whistle, waiting for the game to get good. When Dylan strode out onto the court, I noted how good-looking he was and how confident he seemed, but I wasn't really thinking much more than that. I had been crushing on my friend Ali's older brother Alex. It was a total pipe dream — he was in university already and did not see me as a romantic prospect — but that didn't stop me from hoping I'd grow up faster and morph into some ridiculously hot specimen of his dreams so that the tides would change one day.

Then Dylan rushed the point guard and scored a three pointer in his first five seconds on the court. He smirked a bit and then put his head down and played hard, scoring basket after basket. If his teammates were upset by his ball-hogging, they didn't show it. I think they were as electrified by it as the rest of us.

I remember perking up in my seat, and from then on I couldn't take my eyes off him. Apparently no one else could either; girls took to making signs to display for him at games, and they lined up to try and talk to him afterward. It didn't interest me to become a groupie of his, but I was intrigued by him.

I didn't see him much outside of basketball. Our cheer team practised in the smaller gym while the basketball team practised in the main gym, so we'd see the players running drills while we walked to the other gym. Other than that, we had no classes together since he was in grade twelve and I was a year younger. I never saw him in the cafeteria at lunch or in the hallways in between classes. I wasn't really sure who he hung out with or what else he was interested in.

Then, during a playoff game, our eyes met once. He was normally super focused on the game, so it was a surprise to see him look over. He smiled, and my stomach flopped wildly. I didn't have time to smile back before he was back to concentrating on the game.

"What was that?!" Ali said.

"Yeah — does someone have eyes for Dylan?" Tara added. Her elbow nudged my ribs.

"Looks like Dylan has eyes for you," Ali teased.

"I have no idea what that was," I muttered. I wasn't one to go all gaga just because someone looked at me, but there was something about the intensity of his gaze in that moment that threw me. It was all I could think about. I'd poked fun at the other girls who followed him around like lost puppy dogs, and now I was smitten myself.

At the end of the game, we climbed down from the bleachers and made our way through the crowd to the doors. We passed the team on our way. Coach Wilson was marking something on his clipboard and the players had their heads down around him. I didn't expect Dylan to look up as I passed, but he did, as though he knew where I was the whole time.

"Hi, Annika," he said, flashing me his trademark smirk. I gave him a little wave, trying to keep it cool, but inside I was freaking out.

"Hi, Annika ..." Ali sung out, mocking him. "I didn't realize you two were friends."

We'd never met each other. I knew him because he was Dylan, our school basketball star. Everyone knew him. I had no idea how he knew my name.

"We're not," I whispered back. At least not yet, I thought to myself.

We weren't even out the double doors of the gym when I heard a series of "Congratulations!" and "Great game!" from the people behind me. I turned to see Dylan making his way through the people. Sweat cascaded down his forehead and flushed cheeks. He had this determined look on his face.

I looked forward again, not thinking that he was heading to me.

"Annika!" he called out.

I was so startled — he pulled my elbow and scooted me off to the side of the corridor away from the moving crowd. I saw Ali and Tara stare at me wide-eyed, wondering what was going on. I hoped they'd keep walking so that I could have a moment with Dylan alone.

"Good game," I said simply. Why did he want to talk to me in the first place?

"Yeah, it went okay." He had a wry smile, and two adorable dimples that I'd never noticed before appeared. "I don't want to talk about the game though."

"No?" I stammered. Where was this going?

"We need to go on a date. You and me. Tomorrow."

What?! He was so confident, so sure of himself. As though whatever he asked for he got.

"I barely know you," I said back. It was true. Outside of basketball I did not know a thing about him.

"That's why we're going out tomorrow night. That's gotta change."

I went over my work schedule in my head, knowing full well that I worked Saturday night and my Friday was indeed free. A bunch of us had been planning on going to a movie.

"I've got plans," I told him.

"Not anymore," he said.

"Wait a second — you can't just walk over to me and dictate how I'm going to spend my time. Who do you think you are?" This was crazy. Were we really having this conversation? "You might get your way in basketball, Dylan, but that doesn't work with me." I couldn't even believe the words that were coming out of my mouth.

"Thatta girl," he said laughing. "You are as incredible as I'd hoped you'd be."

I was so flustered I didn't know what to say.

"You're testing me?"

"I love a girl who knows what she wants as much as I do. Now will you give me a chance and go out with me already?" He gave me a puppy dog stare and all I could do was laugh.

"Tomorrow?" It seemed so crazy.

"Yes. Tomorrow. Wanna meet here? Seven?"

"Here?!" It was getting even stranger. If I wasn't getting picked up in a car, and we were meeting at school, was this even a date?

"Yeah. At the doors. I'll see you tomorrow." He winked and turned back faster than he'd come. I stood there trying to process what had just happened.

Ali and Tara ran up to me.

"What was that about?"

"You know that movie tomorrow?" I answered. "Count me out." The girls stood looking at me like I was crazy. "Apparently I'm going on a date instead."

That day feels like ages ago as I watch Dylan standing over the frying pan, ready to flip the sandwiches. He's wearing a Knicks T-shirt and long basketball shorts. The muscles in his calves and biceps are taut and well defined. There's no question that he is strong and handsome. He's even more attractive than when we went on that first date six months ago. I'll never forget that date — how I arrived at the school doors at seven, and how he was waiting on the sidewalk with a lily in his hand.

"For me?" I asked. He bowed a little and handed it to me. He was wearing a grey and white striped button-up shirt, grey dress pants, and leather shoes. He looked like he was ready for a wedding or the club — even though we were too young to go to a club anyhow. I felt a little sheepish in my wool jacket, purple top, dark jeans, and brown leather riding boots, but there was still snow on the ground and we were meeting outside. I didn't exactly know what to expect.

"Come with me," he said. He grabbed my hand and I followed him through the park. On the far end of our schoolyard was a little kids' playground. We headed toward it. Dylan held my hand gently; his hands were soft and warm against my freezing fingers.

Sure enough, we got to the playground and Dylan let go of my hand and sauntered over to the swings. He held one out to me. I giggled and took it from him. He sat on the one next to me, and in seconds the two of us were swinging in unison. It had been years since I'd sat on a swing, and I had forgotten how much fun it was. My hair blew behind me. There was nothing but clear sky and stars as I pumped my legs as hard as I could to match Dylan's. He seemed to spend most of his time studying me as we sailed through the air. If I was supposed to feel self-conscious, I didn't. I was having too much fun and I had to admit I liked the attention. The moonlight made the snow-filled park glisten, and it was beautiful.

Then all of a sudden, Dylan leapt off of his swing when it was as high as it could go. I gasped as I watched him sail through the air. He landed effortlessly and then laughed when he saw my face.

"What? Made you nervous?" he asked. I thought of the snow and ice below and the paltry shock-absorbing abilities of my riding boots and hoped he didn't dare me to do the same. I didn't want to wimp out but I wasn't too sure about being able to nail a successful landing.

Thankfully he walked over to my swing, and caught my leg in mid-air to slow me down. His hand on my leg felt like fire through my jeans, which were stiff with cold. Then he grasped my hands and stopped me. When his hands met mine, I trembled. My breath felt tight in my throat with his touch.

"Ready to go?" he asked.

"Sure," I said. He stuck out his arm for me to loop my arm through his. The snow crunched beneath our feet. We continued down the park path and then onto the nearest street.

"So, how long have you been a cheerleader?" he asked.

"Since grade nine. I've been in dance most of my life, so cheerleading seemed like a good fit I guess." Suddenly I felt a little self-conscious. "How about you?"

"Oh, I've been a cheerleader forever." His face was deadpan. I laughed. "Or maybe just a fan of yours?"

I was so caught off guard. I didn't know what to say. How did he even know who I was?

"We've met before. I don't think you remember?"

I shook my head.

"Laura Ifsham's party. Last year."

Ugh. No wonder I didn't remember him. I barely remembered that party. It was the first time I ever got drunk, and as far as I was concerned, it was going to be the last. I'd gotten so sick that night. Laura's parents were in Mexico, so she threw a big party while they were gone. I had barely drunk alcohol before, and for some reason I decided I was going to drink. I'd even blacked out that night. In hindsight it was so bad I might have had alcohol poisoning. What might I have said or done that made an impression on Dylan?

"Relax," Dylan said, laughing. He must've seen the horror on my face remembering that night. "I know that wasn't the best night for you. At least not toward the end of the night. I helped you when you were lying in the bathroom."

Oh, great. Here's good first-date material. Let's talk about how I helped you when you were puking your guts out last year. That must've been really attractive.

It'd be one thing if I could even remember, but I really couldn't. What else could have happened to me in that state? I was so mad at myself.

"Maybe next time, ease up a little on the booze," Dylan smiled.

"Not to worry. I'm pretty much never drinking again after that," I assured him.

If my parents ever found out about that — I can't imagine. They thought I was just heading over to Laura's for a harmless sleepover. And since she lived around the corner from me, they knew I'd be close by. Thank goodness they hadn't driven by during the night. They would've hauled me out of there so fast if they knew Laura was having a party.

We arrived at the neighbourhood corner store and Dylan headed to the drink machines. He got us two large Styrofoam cups of frothy hot chocolate and a Caramilk bar. We exited the store and sat on a bench by the sidewalk.

"Is this where you take all your dates?" I asked him. It felt like a weird locale for a first date, but I realized I was having a lot of fun with the unexpected.

Dylan didn't answer. He broke up the Caramilk bar and dropped a square into each of our cups.

"This'll make a nice little addition," he assured me. Sure enough, he was right. The chocolate and caramel melted and added extra flavour.

"Thank you for coming with me tonight," he said seriously.

"Thanks for taking me out, or whatever this is," I smiled.

"I do have a car," he assured me. "And next time I'll pick you up."

"What makes you think there'll be a next time?"

"The same reason there was a first time."

"And what was that?"

"That it's time we got to know each other." Dylan took a final swig of his hot chocolate and shot his cup as if it were a basketball toward the garbage can. Not surprisingly, it landed with a satisfying swish into the bin. "Same time tomorrow?"

"Sorry, I can't. I have to work."

"What time are you off?"

"Ten." I wouldn't have been able to hang out with Dylan after work. It would be way too late by the time I got home. My parents would never have gone for that, especially with a boy. It was hard enough to convince them I was going to a movie with friends instead of staying home for family movie night with them.

"Sunday? A daytime date this time?"

My parents might not like this either; they weren't too keen on me dating at all. But I didn't want to say no. I wanted to see Dylan and get to know him. He was spontaneous and fun and this simple date was the best one I'd ever been on.

"Sunday," I agreed.

"When should I pick you up?" he asked.

"You shouldn't. Let's meet here. Two o'clock?"

"Okay …" He seemed surprised. "We can do that. Bring a toboggan."

I laughed.

"You're on," I told him. I turned to walk back toward my house but Dylan pulled me back.

"Annika …" he said. His hand touched mine and I felt tingly everywhere. "You're amazing." His lips brushed my cheek ever so softly, and I melted. He was absolutely right. It was time we got to know each other better.

———

"Your sandwich is ready," Dylan says. He sets the plate in front of me but it lands with a clatter. He's still mad. He takes his sandwich and heads right out the door. I watch as he perches on the edge of the deck to eat. Okay, so he wants to be alone right now. No problem. I wolf down my sandwich, surprised at how hungry I am given that I feel pretty crappy altogether. My head is pounding, and my chest is sore from coughing so much. I know I could use some more puffs from my inhaler.

When I finish eating, I take a couple of puffs of Ventolin, hoping it'll loosen up my chest and help me breathe easier. Dylan is still sitting on the deck. He's done his sandwich, too, but he's staring out into the trees blankly. I start filling the kitchen sink with hot, soapy water to wash the dishes.

I leave the dishes in the empty sink to dry and decide to go upstairs to lie down. I'm hoping a nap will help me to feel better. Or maybe help us both. Maybe I'll wake up and Dylan will be in a better mood, too, and we can start over. I settle into the bed, pulling the thick patchwork quilt over my body and, before I know it, I've drifted off.

DYLAN

The wind is picking up. I can feel it even here, where we're tucked in among the trees. The branches of the evergreens sway wildly at their tops. I can feel goose-bumps prickling my arms, but I sit steadfast on the edge of the deck. Shivering is for wimps.

I want to eat but my sandwich tastes like sandpaper. The fried bread gets caught in my throat, and I have to work to swallow each bite. I thought I was hungry but for some reason I can't fill my stomach. It's tight and twisting within me. If only Annika hadn't lost that fish, we could have avoided all of this. We'd be snuggling on the beach or on the couch or something. I don't even want to look at her right now. If we're going to make this whole thing work we have to be smart about our food. Otherwise how will we survive?

I'll never be able to prove to Anni's parents that I'm the right guy for her. They'll never see that I truly love her and will take care of her … not if I can't even feed us. I watch a squirrel scurry up the side of the tree closest to me. Its grey-brown fur blends right into the trunk. I wouldn't have even seen him if I didn't hear him chattering.

He hides from view and then peers around the corner before chattering once more.

"You a tough guy, now?" I say to him. He disappears from sight again. I continue watching for him. Sure enough, his head appears. He's fixated on me.

"What are you looking at?"

He chatters again, as though he's taunting me. He sticks his face out at me a little further, and I just know he's looking for trouble.

I lean forward to scoop up a pebble and chuck it at him. It hits the trunk, but he's hiding behind it. He gets really loud, as if he's yelling back at me. Just what I need — someone else talking back to me. I grab a few more pebbles and hurl them at the tree. They ping off the bark and clatter to the ground. The squirrel scrambles farther up the tree and leaps to another one. He's too far for me to get him now, and he lets me know it. What I wouldn't give to shut him up right now. I picture my rock knocking him senseless.

That's it. That's the solution. I'll go hunting. Right now. I'll get my gun, head into the woods and get us our food. I'll shoot a nice buck and it'll give us meat for days, and then I won't be worrying about losing a stupid fish.

I stand up from the edge of the deck and brush off my shorts, taking my plate with my uneaten sandwich. I walk into the porch, set my plate down, and grab my knapsack of hunting supplies, my rifle, a hoodie, and a hat. I'm not exactly dressed for hunting in my shorts and sandals, but I don't care. I don't see or hear Annika, and I don't bother to look for her.

I head for the first trail in the trees, just down the road from our cabin. I know this trail goes on for miles. It's often used for quadding and skidooing, but there won't be anyone around right now. I know there's a large clearing about ten minutes away, and if I sit myself there, I'm bound to see something at this time of year. Of course there's no hunting allowed here, but without a soul around, how would anyone know?

As I trudge across the path, I think back to the first time my dad took me hunting. I was about thirteen, and even though my mom wasn't crazy about me going, my dad convinced her that I'd be in good hands and that he'd keep a close eye on me. He was all about safety, and he assured her that nothing would happen. I was so excited to go with him and my Uncle Bill. It felt like I was being let into this exclusive club that represented manhood. I'd begged to go with the two of them all year, thinking I was finally old enough. They usually went hunting at least twice a year. The first time Dad took me I felt like all he did was talk, spouting off every safety rule imaginable. I know it's important to be safe, but didn't he know how excited I was just to try it for myself?

"Hunting is about respecting the animal and the land that you're hunting on," I remember him saying. "We want to hunt ethically. Do you know what 'ethically' means?" I shook my head. "It means following guidelines and obeying the laws around hunting and making responsible choices about what you're doing."

He had explained about using as much of the animal as you can, and how you should try and kill an animal so that it dies quickly with as little pain and suffering as possible. We sat crouched down in a leafy area while he explained the guns, their power and velocity, and how each one worked. The only thing I'd ever used before this was a pellet gun at my grandparents' farm. My dad was teaching me how to use the rifle, and he was going to use a handgun, a .44 Magnum S&W 629 Stealth Hunter, his prized possession he'd inherited from his dad.

"This here, Dylan, requires more skill and accuracy than a rifle. With a gun like this one has to be a pretty good shot, and be able to get closer to the prey, to take the animal cleanly and humanely." He went on to explain the finer details of the gun and told me I was never to use it, that I'd have to wait until I was older and had considerable shooting experience. I was fine with that. The rifle felt like plenty of gun for me and I had to admit I was intimidated by the size and feel of it.

I wonder how my dad would feel knowing that I have his beloved handgun in my backpack right now. It probably wouldn't take him long normally to realize it was missing, now that it's hunting season, but he'll definitely check the gun case when he realizes I'm gone.

The ground alternates between soft, cushiony moss and tough, twisted tree roots covered in crunchy pine needles. I'm mostly sheltered from the wind. My heart speeds up with every step. I study the lush green landscape that forms a canopy around me. God, I love this area. My backpack feels heavy on my shoulders. I pull it closer to my back hoping to shift the weight a bit. The path leads me exactly to where I want to be, a clearing that angles upward. If I make it over the hill, I can crouch down and take aim downward until the clearing meets forest again.

There are many fresh rubs and scrapes at the edge of the clearing. Just as I suspected, there has been a lot of activity here.

2:00 P.M.

ANNIKA

My dreams come in fitful starts and stops. Mostly there are a mix of the people I love: Dylan and me, either gloriously happy or fighting dirty, spouting angry words at each other. My parents, either hugging me tightly and professing their love for me or berating me for running off with Dylan. Roxy, jumping all over me and licking my face or growling at me. Even my brother Mark shows up, smiling at me or doing something mean. The dreams alternate between really good or really depressing and I can't make sense of them. I wake to find my hair slick with sweat and sticking to my head and neck. Despite the medication I took, this fever just won't let up. I set my head back down and hope that sleep will bring the relief I need.

DYLAN

I hear the sounds of twigs breaking ahead of me. I'm momentarily stunned. A big buck is standing not forty feet from me right on the grassy hill. He's within my range for sure. There aren't any obstructions. I'm set up for a near-perfect shot. His head is down. He doesn't know I'm here. My heart quickens.

One shot and he's mine. I know it. But he's in the worst spot. I mean, if I start shooting up toward the hill at him, my lead is going to carry well beyond him. I can almost hear my dad telling me to walk away from this one.

"It's not safe, Dyl," he'd advise. "You don't know who or what's beyond that hill. This isn't a good angle."

Of course he'd want to ruin this for me. My chance at a perfect shot right now and he'd squash it. This is too good to pass up. It's meat for weeks.

"Sorry, Dad. Gotta eat."

I set my rifle down beside me and gingerly swing my backpack around so that I can open it and get the handgun without startling him. My heart is hammering in my chest knowing that with a buck this close, I'll finally be able to use that gun. I slide it out as carefully as I can and position myself.

"Please don't see me," I think to myself. If he looks up, he'll dart away before I can get a clear shot.

My hands slip a bit on the cold metal. Beads of sweat form on my forehead. I've got to get this shot and get this buck back to the cabin as soon as I can. As soon as I line up the shot, my finger presses the trigger. The shot rings out, sending birds flying in all directions from the trees. The gun kicks back at me. It whacks me on the heel of my hand and I realize how much less it would hurt if I'd worn gloves. The buck drops immediately.

"Yes!" I say aloud. I have him. I start to make my way to him but then he makes a loud, barking sound that unnerves me and he stumbles back to his feet. He starts to run off again, stumbling in a zig zag pattern. I can see the blood dripping from him. He makes it down the other side of the hill, so I run up after him. I can't let him get away.

I see bright gobs of blood splattered all over the grass. He's already made it past the clearing. I know I got him good, so he can't go too far, can he? I continue to track him. The blood trail starts to thin out as I trace his steps.

"Another tough guy," I mutter. I know I had him. That shot was textbook perfect.

Again I can hear my dad's voice. "What are you doing, Dyl? If your shot doesn't make for a quick kill it shouldn't be taken."

"Shut up," I mutter under my breath. My dad's not here and I know what I'm doing.

This buck is not going to win. Not today. My eyes dart around the forest floor, hoping to see my deer laid out on the ground somewhere. Instead I hear voices in the distance.

"No!" I yell inside my head. This is the last thing I need. This is definitely a no-hunting zone and I've lost my kill. No one can see me here or know what's happened. They probably heard the shot. Of course. I run to my left, deeper into the trees. I've got to find a place to hide and hope that the voices pass.

My breaths are coming in ragged gasps by the time I find a small thicket to hide behind. I can only hope that I'm far enough away. The voices are getting closer, and then I see them. Two men about my dad's age, both wearing coveralls and boots. They are walking with purpose. I watch their faces turn in every direction. They are definitely looking for something.

Their footsteps get louder and I know they're getting closer and closer to me. The sweat that had initially started on my forehead trickles down my back in a steady stream. I try not to breathe loudly.

"What kind of fool shoots out here?" one of the men says.

"I don't know, but the police are going to hear about this," the other one says. "This is my land, and when I get my hands on the dumbass shooting so close to a public beach ... god help him."

I can make out their words plain as day. They continue toward the clearing, and I don't dare move again until they are a long way past me. Eventually they'll see the blood trail clearly and they'll be able to follow it right to where the buck went down.

I stand and decide to race deeper into the woods, hoping I'll still find my prize at the end of this. I veer further east, closer to where I know the water is and further from the direction the men came from. I feel clammy. My clothes are soaked with sweat.

I just need to find that animal and I can get out of here and head back to the cabin. Where is he? I have to find him. We'll be set if I can bring this animal back. I crouch down while I search. Those men cannot find me.

Looking around I see that there are shrubs with visibly flattened branches, as though something has trampled through them. I'm on the right track!

I slink through the foliage with renewed vigour. With luck, that buck will be close. A gust of wind sends a loud whoosh through the air and I jump from the sudden rush of noise. Every part of me feels tense and tight. And then I see him. He's lying on his left side, unmoving. As I approach I see that he's dead. His mouth hangs open; his head is limp against the forest floor.

His golden hide is marred with deep ruby spatters and an oozing wound that I see now got him in the lungs. A perfect hit just like I suspected. I feel a swell of pride. Whether I should have taken the shot or not, I nailed him right where I wanted to, and here he is, ready for the taking. The only thing is he's probably a good two hundred pounds and he's way further from the trail than I planned. Hooking my rope to him and dragging him back probably won't work so well — not with the size of this one and those men out looking for me now. I need a vehicle. But of course my car is sitting on the freaking highway, the motor most likely burned out, and I've got no way to fix it.

That's the way things work for me. The world is always crashing down on me, trying to take me down with it. I've been tested time and time again. From my parents not giving a shit about me to having so-called friends betray me. Teachers don't give a crap about me except to breathe down my neck. Only Coach Wilson has shown interest in me, but that's only because I'm his star player.

Annika's parents think I'm bad news for their girl. They have no idea how much I love and care for her. How I'm a good guy. If they'd just give me a chance.... They've raised a smart and beautiful daughter, but they can't see that either. If she loves me, can't they take her word for the kind of guy I am? Why doesn't her opinion count?

Part of the problem is that once you're labelled, good luck trying to shed whatever people think of you. I remember when my old friend Travis and I snuck into the school's maintenance room to smoke the leftover butt of a cigarette that Travis found on the playground. We were, like, eight years old, and when Mr. Pattison, the caretaker, caught us in the corner of the room, the way he jumped and screamed wildly at us you'd think we'd just doused the building in gasoline and were holding a match up in the air about to drop it.

From then on it's like the teachers had an opinion of me. They'd watch me carefully in their classes and they didn't seem to joke with me like they did with the other kids. I'd try to be funny, thinking the class clown approach would win me some likeability points, but that only seemed to work with the kids. Most teachers just stuck it to me harder.

That's also about the time my parents signed me up for basketball, hoping that sports would keep me focused and out of trouble, and that I'd learn how to play on a team. I took to it right away and have been playing ever since.

I'm not a bad guy. I care a lot about people. I'm a passionate person. I stand up for what I believe in and if I think something isn't right I voice my opinion. You don't have to agree with me. I just want my voice to be heard. That's one thing I've learned. If people are always trying to push you down, you have to fight twice as hard and be twice as loud to make sure you rise above.

3:00 P.M.

ANNIKA

I sit up in bed and listen for Dylan, but it is eerily quiet. I can hear the wind whipping through the trees outside and the odd creak from the walls of the cabin but there are no inside sounds. I cough, another long, drawn-out bout that lasts almost a full minute, and I'm panting by the end of it. I reach for my inhaler and take several puffs, hoping it takes the weight off of my chest so that I can breathe better. I haven't felt this sick in a long time and part of me wants to cry because I feel so awful. All of a sudden I think of my mom and I wish she were here. She'd know what to do to help me feel better. And even though her constant hovering into my life is annoying, when I'm sick she's who I think of.

I check my phone and there are no new texts. I thought there would be twelve more frantic texts from her, so seeing that there isn't even one makes me feel a bit lonely. Dylan was so mad earlier. I know he's worried about our future, but we'll be okay. We'll get settled and established and we have each other. I just wish he wouldn't get so angry so quick. This happens when he's stressed out, and sometimes no matter what I do to try to calm him, his temper flares even further, like adding fuel to a fire.

I have to tell him it'll be okay. Make him see that we'll be just fine. He's been gone for quite a while now, and a pit is forming in my stomach. I feel really uneasy knowing that Dylan is so angry and having no idea where he is or when he'll return.

I gaze around at this cozy place and I can't help but realize that our homecoming is nothing like I thought it would be so far. I didn't imagine us bickering or Dylan getting so mad. I mean, I figured we'd have our share of issues like any other couple, but that maybe it would come later. We've just arrived and this is supposed to be a happy time.

I walk around the cabin. My teeth start to chatter a bit and I rub my arms vigorously. This stupid fever just doesn't want to let up. I keep glancing at the road, hoping to see Dylan walk up, but all I see is a quiet gravel road and trees swaying in the wind. I want to give him a hug and let him know that everything will be okay. That we're in this together and that I'm not going anywhere.

I think back to my own family's lake trips. I think of the boring car rides up to whatever campsite Dad had managed to book for us last minute, since that's how we always did things — spur-of-the-moment — and how I'd listen to music most of the way up so that I could have some space and be alone with my thoughts. We'd get to the site and after that it was all hands on deck to get the tent up and our gear unpacked. Mom always over-packed; she wanted to be prepared for practically anything. We'd tease her for bringing so much stuff, but at the same time it was comforting knowing that whatever we needed, Mom had probably brought it. We'd get the blankets and sleeping bags piled into the tent and all I'd want to do is curl up with a book, the fresh air flowing through the tent. I picture us sitting around the fire, telling jokes, reading ghost stories … the hundreds of marshmallows we roasted. I think of us playing with a Nerf football in the water, always trying to throw it a little short so that it would land in front of the person and water would splash in their face. When we were pretty little, Mark and I would have chicken fights — each of us on a parent's shoulders trying to wrestle the other off into the water. It was always a fun time. Mom and Dad were so relaxed at the lake. They were way more lenient, too. We could roam on our own and go exploring without Mom panicking about where we were so much. I just remember it being so happy.

I thought that this was how it was going to be with Dylan. We got off to a rocky start, but I have to believe that it will be all right. I can turn this around. I'll go outside and start a nice fire for us in the fire pit outside. We can pull out some of the patio chairs and sit around the flames. They'll keep us warm in this ugly weather.

I slip on my shoes, matches in hand, and close the cabin door behind me. I can tell the wind is strong by the way the treetops sway, even though we're mostly protected from it here in the trees. The woodshed is piled high beneath the tarp that covers it. I look for some smaller twigs that I can burn first.

I pull off the metal grill that covers the fire pit and make a neat pile with the twigs and leaves I've collected. Everything is nice and dry, so I should be able to start a fire easily. I light the first match and hold it carefully up to one of the twigs. The wood glows orange and smokes a bit before lighting into a small flame. I blow softly on the flame, just like my dad taught me, and watch as the flame spreads quickly to the other pieces. In mere seconds, I have lit a small fire. I smile even though my lungs burn from the smoke. I quickly put a few more twigs on the pile to help the fire grow. I know I have to establish this a while longer before I can add any big pieces of wood. My dad would be so proud of me right now. "First try!" I say out loud. I wish Dylan was here to see this. He'd know I have some skills too and that we were in this together. The smoke billows up into my face and I cough for several minutes until I'm wheezing heavily once more. I add some wood to the now-established fire and then go back into the cabin to get my inhaler. The fire will be nice and strong and I'm looking forward to sitting with Dylan in front of it. I glance at the road but there is still no sign of him.

DYLAN

People underestimate me. They have no idea what a fighter I am, what a strong person I've become. They'll never know my struggle. No one has had to overcome like I have. It's why I'm sitting in the forest, my hands covered in fresh animal blood as I field dress this deer. It's why I will get it home to my girlfriend so that I can provide for her. It's why we've planned this whole thing, being self-sufficient and capable, and I won't let her down. It's why I've learned so many skills — so that I can take care of myself. So I don't have to rely on anybody but myself.

I pull out my knife and the bag I've brought with me. My limited supplies make this hunt a challenge, but I'll make it work. I press the knife gently across the buck's abdomen, careful not to puncture too far. I know I should have a bag with me to put the insides in. I'll have to bury them and hope that I get out of here before those men come back or a bear smells the flesh of this guy. The metallic smell of blood is enough to make me gag, but I have to do this as quickly and quietly as I can.

I manage to get him cleaned out enough so that I can get him tied up with my rope; then I can get him back to the cabin. I'm slick with sweat — it streams down my face and burns my eyes and I have to squeeze my eyes shut periodically to try and take the sting away.

I scoop up a pile of leaves and stray branches to cover the guts of the buck. It's not ideal and those men will probably find them, especially if they bring a dog out here to search, but it's all I've got right now. I use my feet to slide some stray branches over the area, too. I've got to try to make my way back *now*.

Hoisting the rope over my shoulder, I drag the deer behind me. It takes a lot of my strength to get him gliding over the forest floor, especially with all of the bumps and roots scattered throughout this area. Blood drops expose our trail. There is crunching and the sounds of twigs snapping beneath us, so I stop and listen for voices or other noises but I hear nothing. I tug harder, trying to move more quickly, and my arms throb and ache from the strain.

By the time I reach the clearing, I am so slick with sweat that the rope keeps slipping through my hands. I stop to wipe them on my shorts but they are practically dripping with sweat on their own. The rifle is also slung over my shoulder and it bangs repeatedly into my body as I move. The buck is slack-jawed; his eyes are empty, like two black beady disks. I stop and look around. I have to be absolutely sure that I can make it through this clearing back to the path to the road without anyone seeing me, or I'm toast.

The forest is quiet at the moment. I hear some birds overhead, but otherwise all I can hear is my heart pounding through my chest and the sound of my panting breaths. I think I'm good to go.

I make a break for the path over the hill. It's all I can do to drag this buck up the hill, never mind do it quickly. I can feel the adrenaline pulsing through my body. My arms and legs tremble and I stumble a few times as I try to scramble up the hill. I fall on my butt at the top.

"C'mon, you piece of shit," I mutter at the giant hunk of meat. I start pulling him up toward me from my seated position on the hill, using my legs to push myself upward while my arms drag the carcass along. I can barely breathe. I manage to get him to the top when I hear them.

"There he is!" It's the men who were looking for me before. They break out into a run. I freeze momentarily. The only thing I can do is run. I drop the rope holding my buck and turn south. Hopefully I can lose them and make it back to the cabin to hide. I leap down into the trees. The uneven ground threatens to trip me up but I can't risk falling. I have to keep running as fast as I can. I was already exhausted from dragging the deer, but a new burst of adrenaline helps me continue on. I can hear them yelling after me, though I can't make out what they're saying. I don't need to know what they're saying.

I speed through the trees, branches slicing across my arms and chest, snapping off and flying in the air behind me. It's loud and crackling, but I can't help it. If I can veer back toward the cleared path, I can run without being heard as much. I glance behind me and I can't see them, but I can hear them hollering.

My deer is sitting on the top of the hill at the clearing, fresh for their taking. The thought pisses me off to no end. It was my kill. My shot. And now these jerks will benefit. I'm sure they've got enough meat stuffed into their freezers to last for months. This buck means nothing to them.

I see the path to my right, so I pick up the pace to get there. I can barely breathe, but I can't stop. My steps become much quieter on the path and without any brush to slow me down, I run full tilt. I'll be back at the cabin soon and Annika and I can stay hidden inside. Those men won't have a clue where to find me.

4:00 P.M.

ANNIKA

A figure comes running down the road so fast I'd miss him if it weren't for the heavy panting I hear. As the figure gets closer I see that it's Dylan. I jump from my seat and race toward him. He's red-faced, dripping with sweat, and he's not slowing down. He looks as though he's about to run right past me like I'm invisible.

"Dylan?!" I exclaim.

He starts shaking his head at me and waving me off, like I shouldn't get near him. Something is very wrong. I feel it in the pit of my stomach and I wonder what's got him like this. Then I glance down at the rest of him, and I see that he's covered in blood. It's dried onto his hands, his arms, his clothes.

"Are you okay?!" I shriek. "Are you bleeding?!" Tears start to form in my eyes. "Dylan?!" I shriek again. He's not even responding to me.

"I'm ... not ... bleeding." He's trying to catch his breath. "Get ... in ... the ... house!"

"Why? What's happened?" Bile rises up my throat. Was he attacked by something? Why are we in danger?

Dylan notices the fire and starts swearing.

"Put that out!" he yells. My feet stay firmly in place. I don't know what to make of any of this. What could be wrong with the fire?

"Now!"

I stay rooted in the same spot while Dylan starts running for the cabin. Moments later he comes back with a bucket of water.

"Get in the cabin," he says. I don't move. In one swift motion, Dylan douses the fire with the water and it sizzles loudly. Heavy smoke swirls toward the sky. He's clearly panicked about something. I know I should run into the cabin, but he's scaring me and for some reason I can't seem to budge.

"God, Anni, move!" Dylan grabs my arm and pulls me so hard I yelp. I stumble after him toward the cabin, and he practically shoves me through the door.

"Dylan, what is going on?!" I yell back.

"We have to stay in here," he says softly. He's bent over with his hands on his knees. He is still trying to catch his breath.

"Why do you have blood on you? You're not hurt?"

"I'm not hurt," he assures me.

"Whose blood is it?" I'm not sure I want to know.

"I was just out hunting. Bringing us back some meat is all."

It can't be that easy. He wouldn't be racing back like that and he definitely didn't have the meat with him. And why would he go hunting without telling me?

"You went out into the woods and didn't tell me? How would I know what to do if you didn't return?" A flash of anger comes over me. We have barely settled into this place. Taking off into the woods without saying anything to me seems irresponsible.

"Look, Annika ... I wouldn't have had to go into the woods to get us meat in the first place if you hadn't lost that fish."

"Excuse me?"

"Well, we need food somehow."

My eyes grow wide. "Dylan, we just got here. We have plenty of food and plenty of time to get more. What's a fish going to change? I thought we were roasting hot dogs tonight anyway?"

"I want to make sure we have enough food."

"Well, I want to make sure I have *you*," I tell him. But I know this is about more than food. This is also about Dylan needing space and going out into the woods to work his anger out.

And this scares me a little. We've only just arrived and already he's needing space. I don't want to ask where the animal is or how the hunting turned out. But I have to know what's going on.

"Why were you running?"

Dylan bites his lip and stays silent.

"There was this bear that came while I was getting my buck ready to transport. Instead of staying with the buck, she decided to chase me." He clears his throat. "Ever been chased by a bear, Anni?"

"Of course I haven't. It's one of the things I was most scared of, coming here!"

"I guarantee you'd run like that if a bear was chasing you, too."

I picture a bear on Dylan's heels and the thought makes my stomach flop. No wonder he looked so crazed when he got here. I embrace him and squeeze him close to me.

"Thank god you're okay!" I kiss his cheek and he wraps his arms around me firmly. He's finally calming down and settling into me. He kisses me back.

"Let's get you cleaned up," I say. I find a face cloth and wet it with warm water. I wring it out and bring it to Dylan's face. He's got a combination of sweat, dirt, and what is most likely blood streaking his cheeks. He sighs when I caress his face with the cloth.

"Thanks, Anni." His voice breaks.

"I've got you," I say gently. I'm stunned to see tears in Dylan's eyes.

"I'm sorry for before," I say. "I really didn't mean to lose the fish."

"It happens."

"Please don't go back into the woods without telling me," I tell him.

"Okay. I won't," Dylan replies.

"Don't worry about food," I assure him. "We'll be okay."

"I'm trying, Anni. I just want everything to be perfect for us." Dylan's shoulders shake with emotion. Tears cascade down his cheeks now.

"Things *are* perfect. We have each other." I wipe the grime from his face, along with the warm tears that follow. His tense shoulders drop, and then his tears flow openly.

"Yes, we have each other," he whispers. I continue to stroke his cheeks with the cloth, absorbing his tears. He leans into my shoulder and I feel the weight of what he holds in his mind as he cries. How do I convince him that the perfection he is seeking isn't possible? That life will have its ups and downs and that what makes it perfect is riding the waves together?

DYLAN

God, it feels so good to have Annika hold me like this. I can feel her love for me in every gentle, sweet movement she makes. I know I scared her, running back here covered in blood. She bought the bear story, so hopefully I can put this hunting fiasco to rest. Forget about it and move on. My buck is still waiting for me, though. As long as those dumb old guys haven't hauled him away for themselves. They probably have. Greedy assholes.

Maybe I should go back and try and find him, drag him back. No, there'd be no use. Those meddling men will be watching for me, guaranteed. It's best that I just go out on a new hunt in a day or two once things have quieted down around here.

I pull Annika even closer to me. She's so warm and comforting; she makes all of the bad feelings disappear. I have to just focus on her and our new life together. Just relax and take this all in with her. Why can't I relax? Why is this nothing like I planned? What if I'm wrong? What if she's just waiting for the right time to leave? What if she thinks this has all been a mistake?

When my nose brushes Annika's neck, I feel how warm she is. I nestle my cheek against her, too, and realize that she's practically radiating heat. I pull back to look at her. She looks exhausted. Rings have formed around her eyes, and I realize that she's probably sicker than I thought.

"Anni, you're burning up," I tell her.

"I'm okay," she says softly, but I can tell she doesn't feel well at all.

"Give me a few minutes to clean up," I say. "Then I'll hold you." I run upstairs to grab a towel so I can take a quick shower and change out of these filthy, bloody clothes. Annika sits on the edge of the couch, watching me. She looks more relaxed and eager for me to return so I decide to shower as fast as I can. When I step into the bathroom, I almost gasp at my reflection in the mirror. I'm a mess. My hair is tangled and standing in every direction. Dirt and blood are caked into my hairline. My eyes are wide and wild, and they threaten to betray the racing thoughts in my mind.

What if those men show up here? What will I do? What will I say? What will Annika think? She knows I was hunting, but she has no idea what really happened out there. If she learns the truth, she'll be really upset with me. She likes to follow rules. She does things by the book. Well, usually, until she agreed to run away with me. That wasn't exactly in her plans. If her parents would stop telling her to break up with me, well, maybe we'd have been able to stick around. It's their fault we had to go in the first place.

Annika won't understand what a perfect shot I had, how I couldn't possibly let the buck get away. She'll know from the anger on those men's faces that what I did was wrong. And then I'll never get her to agree to go hunting with me. Why couldn't those men have minded their own business anyhow? I wasn't hurting anyone (except the buck), and technically I was shooting game for our survival. I stare at my reflection and try to calm myself. My girl is waiting for me in the next room.

The shower is like a warm, soothing embrace. The soft pelting of the water washes away all the fear I am carrying. I quickly lather myself up and then rinse off, eager to get back to Annika. When I get back to the living room, she's still on the couch. Her knees are pulled up to her chest and she's hugging her legs. She looks so worn out.

"Aw, babe," I whisper. I sit beside her and pull her into me. She coughs again, and her whole body vibrates with the force of it. She nestles into my neck and curls into me. I rub her back with my hand. "Can you take more medicine?"

She shakes her head. "Not yet."

Annika is quite sick. She is breathing more heavily now and there's a slight wheeze when she breathes out. She doesn't have a lot of energy, and she's still super warm to the touch.

We snuggle together for several minutes. The feel of her in my arms is incredible. Like I've found my home.

"I love you, Anni…."

"I love you too, Dyl," she answers softly. Her eyes are closed. I wonder how close she is to drifting off.

"No, really, I love you," I say pointedly.

I wait for an answer but nothing comes. I look down at her face and see a small smile forming on her lips. Good. She heard me. I need her to know. I need her to feel my love, to know that I'll do anything for her. I need her to feel secure in my love for her so that she never doubts it. I will take care of her. I will. I will prove it to her parents that I've got what it takes to be with their daughter.

Annika never had to prove herself to my parents. Or at least not to my dad. I never really wanted them to meet, but Annika insisted on it. I didn't really want her coming by my house. I told her that I spent as little time there as possible. We invited my dad to a coffee shop downtown, just a block from his office. I thought it would be a good idea since my dad rarely took his lunch break; he'd probably be counting the minutes before he could stand up and leave and get back to what he does best: working.

I was nervous about the whole thing. I didn't want Annika to be fooled by my dad and his friendly demeanour. She'd think I was overreacting about how tough it was to have a relationship with my parents. Annika practically skipped down the sidewalk toward the coffee shop. When we walked through the doors, my dad was seated at a corner table, his navy suit and striped yellow tie neatly pressed. He smiled warmly at us and stood to greet us.

"Dad, this is Annika. Annika, Allan."

He pulled Annika in for a strong hug and told her what a pretty girl she was. Annika blushed and I wanted to dump coffee onto my dad and walk out. He could at least limit his womanizing enough to not include his son's girlfriend.

He reached out to me and I stepped back so that his arm fell short of my shoulder. He paused, clearly surprised by my chilliness toward him. I pulled out a chair for Annika, and she sat down and began chattering away.

The two of them seemed to hit it off. My dad's a big history buff, so as soon as he found out that Annika liked history, the two of them couldn't stop talking. I pretty well just sat there listening to them.

"You studied history in university?" Annika asked him.

"Sure did. Considered a career in it too, but wasn't sure it would get me too far," Dad admitted. "In the end I went into commerce after my bachelor's degree. Do you know what you want to do?"

"I'm considering dentistry," Annika told him. "But it's still really early for me to decide something like that. I have to finish high school first." Dad's face lit up in a way I'd never seen before. He glanced over at me and I could tell he was impressed.

"Wow," was all he said, still looking at me. I knew what he was thinking. He was shocked that a smart girl with some serious future plans might ever be with someone like me. He didn't have to say it. It was plain as day.

"Maybe you can help Dylan figure out what he'd like to do," my dad chuckled.

Just then, I wanted to walk out. I mean, how insulting to call your son out in front of his girlfriend the first time you meet her? Who does that?

"I've got a career, Dad," I shot back. "Working with good ol' Uncle Bill." My dad pretty well forced me to work that job — if I didn't, I had to move out.

We looked each other squarely in the face. My dad looked like he wanted to say something but then held back. Annika seemed to think nothing was wrong and continued chatting. When my dad finally stood up and announced that he had to leave, Annika rose to give him another hug.

"Pleasure to meet you, Annika," he said warmly.

"And you too, Mr. Sopick."

"Dylan, you have a lovely girl here," he said, putting his hand on my shoulder before I could pull away. I flinched a little under his touch and I wondered if he felt it.

"Just wondering what she's doing with me, right Dad?" I countered. My dad pretended to look stunned and shook his head.

"C'mon, Dyl, don't be like this …"

"No really. Say what you mean. You wonder what she sees in me, right? Your son with no real job, no real future. At least as far as you can see. You can't just trust that I'll find my way. That I might actually make something of myself. But carpentry doesn't count, does it? It's not good enough for you."

"Dylan, enough," Dad said sharply.

"You're right. This has been enough." I threw a ten dollar bill onto the table and walked straight out of the coffee shop. I strode down the sidewalk and right back to the parking space where my car was.

Annika came running toward the car a short time later. "Dylan, what was that about?"

"There you go. You've met my dad."

"I didn't think he said anything bad. Or at least I don't think he meant to," Annika said.

"Sure. You meet him for like five minutes and you think he's Mr. Wonderful. Of course you would. My family will put their best foot forward meeting someone. It's all part of that all-important first impression. You haven't lived with them, grown up with them. You'll see."

"Okay, I get it," Annika said.

"No, you don't. My parents haven't been there for me the way yours have."

I never brought Annika back to see my dad. It was just easier. He never stopped asking about her though, and I know he would've liked it if I brought her around. I considered bringing her around to meet my mom, but I'd already told her that my mom lived across the country and was remarried with a baby on the way. The lie came out so quickly and easily, I had no way to take it back. The truth felt more embarrassing, and I didn't want to pretend to Annika that I had a perfect family when all of these years that my parents stayed together were really a sham. I guess I was giving my mom the future I wish she had. Someone who loved and cared about her enough to be faithful to her and give her a fresh start. And I gave her the story of a baby on the way — one that would grow up to be a good kid and not give her so much trouble like her current son, who had started disobeying teachers and pulling pranks. I'd give her a son who didn't want to pummel his dad. A kid who didn't spend a lot of his time trying to figure out how to either prove himself to others or find ways to escape life altogether. I run my fingers down the inside of my left arm. The three-inch scar is raised and bumpy. It's only one of the markers of my attempts to escape life, but it's a story that Annika doesn't know about.

Even though our second date was an afternoon date, I was so full of good energy the rest of the day that I couldn't sit still. I decided to go for a drive. I figured Annika would be in bed, especially since it was after eleven and her parents were so strict. Just being on the same street as her felt like I was connecting with her, so I drove to her house and parked across the street.

I stared up at her family's beige two-storey, and to my surprise a figure shifted on the front porch. It was too dark to make out who it was, so part of me wanted to hit the gas and drive away as fast as I could before her parents saw me. They'd wonder why I was there so late. But then my phone dinged with a text message.

Why are you here? I'm sitting on the porch! 11:14 p.m.

Just missing you. I wanted to be closer to you. 11:14 p.m.

That's sweet. 11:14 p.m.

Is it safe to come closer? 11:15 p.m.

I watched the figure stand and look through the front window and the door.

Coast is clear. 11:15 p.m.

I smiled and turned the engine off. I put my keys in my pocket so they wouldn't make so much noise and I practically tiptoed across the street to the Diettys' front porch.

Annika looked radiant. Her hair was piled up in a loose bun on the top of her head, and she was wearing flannel pajamas and fuzzy slippers.

"Come sit," she smiled, patting the empty spot beside her on the patio loveseat. I kept looking into the house, hoping that her parents wouldn't see me.

"Relax. My parents are in bed," she assured me.

"I had a great time today, Annika." I took her hand in mine.

"I did, too," she said. She blushed and it made my stomach do flip-flops. She stared down at our hands intertwined and then released her hand from mine. She turned my arm over and ran her fingertips gently over my scar and asked me what had happened. I told her I had cut my wrist open on a raised wire while I was climbing over a chain-link fence. I wanted that scar to be from something as simple as a fence. And maybe if I said it enough I'd come to believe it as the truth. She caressed it softly and gave me a sympathetic stare, and then she showed me the scar on her index finger that she got slicing veggies at her grandma's house for a family reunion. We held hands for a long time before deciding to make wishes on the twinkling sky above. I kissed her then, and, as much as I wanted to stay with her all night, I told her it was time for me to go so she could get to bed. She put her arms around my neck and looked into my eyes, and all I could think was how beautiful she was and how this girl was the best thing to ever happen to me.

My mom would have loved Annika. I could picture the two of them having tea and flipping through photo albums of me as a kid, gushing at the pictures just like you see in the movies. But the picture wouldn't be accurate. It would showcase a happy family. And while we were a happy family in the early years, the facade has gone on long enough.

A few years ago when I was getting in trouble for mouthing her off, my mom admitted that she knew about the other women in my dad's life.

"Why are you still with him?" My words were laced with disgust. I had walked in to her wiping away tears at the dining room window, staring out at the backyard with a blank look in her eyes. She had tried to straighten herself and act like nothing was wrong, but I knew better. My dad hadn't been home in several days and I knew he was sleeping on the couch most nights when he was home. She didn't answer.

"Seriously. He doesn't care about you or me."

"He does, Dylan," my mom said. "He loves us very much. It's not that easy."

"What? Keeping it in your pants for your wife? Being home and being a real dad to your kid? It can't be that hard. Most dads on the planet manage just fine...."

"We will always be a family," my mom said. I wondered if she was trying to convince herself when she said it. "You have always been the best thing to ever happen to us," she continued, coming toward me. Her arms were outstretched like she wanted to pull me into them. I loved her and I wanted to hug her, but I also wanted to push her away. Watching her get hurt over and over again by a cheating husband was not a good example of family, no matter how good her intentions were in staying and trying to keep us together. Maybe what parents think is best for their child really isn't.

"No!" I said, guarding myself from her touch. She tried to pull me in but I was already so much taller than her, it was easy to shut her out.

It's years later and I'm tired of my mom pretending that we're still that family, even though she knows my dad acts like a part-time husband, and that he checked out long ago. I'm tired of him hiding behind his work as an excuse instead of being with us. I'm tired of her allowing him to be shared with others. I'm tired of being disappointed in him. It's just easier to be mad and hate him for what he's done.

I'll never treat Annika the way my dad has treated my mother. I'll be so devoted and faithful to her, she'll never doubt my love for her. I'll show him what real love looks like. Annika's silence gives way to a soft snore. She's fallen asleep in my arms. I continue rubbing her back, grateful that she's resting. Maybe she needs a doctor. I mean, I thought it was just a little flu bug of some sort, but she seems really sick. The nearest town is about thirty minutes away. It has a little hospital. Except how would I get her there? Once again, I'm showing that I can't be the guy she needs. I can't even get her to medical care without asking for assistance.

Would her parents take her to a hospital if she was this sick? I know with asthma you're not supposed to fool around when someone is having trouble breathing. Just listening to her soft, high-pitched wheezes as she's sleeping is enough to unnerve me. I try to imagine what her mom would do.

Annika's phone buzzes with another text. And then another. And another. I can see her phone sticking out of her pants pocket. She doesn't move a muscle. The buzzing does nothing to wake her. I decide to slide her phone out of her pocket to see who might be calling.

Annika, are you still with Elise? 4:53 p.m.

It's her mom. Like there was any doubt. Plus there are four missed calls, all from her parents.

Elise? Who is Elise? I scroll back and read what Annika wrote to her mom earlier. So she's making up some bogus story for now. She hasn't told her parents where she is.

The next text is from Paul. Just seeing the letters of his name makes me want to punch him out.

Hey Anni. Been a while. Going to stop by tomorrow. 4:54 p.m.

What the hell does Paul want with Annika? I know they are next-door neighbours and childhood friends, but can't you just wave at each other and get on with your day? I debate writing something back to him telling him off; at first I decide against it. I'll put an end to that one in person. But then I think of him trying to get my girl and realize it can't wait.

You better watch your back. Stay away from Anni. 4:56 p.m.

I scroll through her messages briefly and am relieved that I don't see any other guys' names as recent texts. I mean, I know she loves me, but Annika is an amazing girl. I'm sure tons of guys would try to take her from me if they had the chance.

Annika shifts a bit and I quickly set down her phone. I don't want her thinking I'm snooping. I don't know why I'm doing it. I trust her. I really do. It's everyone else I don't trust. Maybe it's best if I just hide her phone somewhere. It might take her a while to find out it's missing since she's sick, and then we'll get a break from these people trying to run her life. I shut her phone down and shove it into the back cushions of the couch until it's squeezed firmly down the gap in the couch frame. It'll be tough to find it in there. There's something immensely satisfying about silencing that phone.

5:00 P.M.

ANNIKA

I wake with a start. Dylan is practically throwing me off of him. I stumble toward the floor from the couch and turn to see what's happening. Dylan is turned toward the window. An RCMP patrol car is driving slowly down the road. Dylan's eyes are fixed on the car.

"You think he's out looking for that bear?" I say, rubbing sleep from my eyes.

"What?" Dylan says, distracted.

"The bear?" I repeat. "They must be looking for the bear. Someone else must've seen the bear roaming too."

"Yeah," Dylan says quietly.

"Well, let's go flag him down and tell him your story! You know which way the bear was headed!" I start for the door. It's better for everyone if this bear gets caught before someone gets hurt.

"NO!" Dylan yells. "Stay here!"

I jump. "Dyl, what's the deal?" He's the perfect person to help with this.

"Stay here, Anni, please." Dylan's voice is shaky. In fact, I look closer and his hands are shaking a bit, too.

"Are you okay?" I ask. Dylan turns to me and he's got tears running down his cheeks again. He's not okay. Not at all. He looks back to the window. I go to him and grab both of his hands.

"Dylan, I'm here. I'm not going anywhere." I try to turn his face back to me but he won't budge. He's fixated on the police car outside. It isn't until the car continues down the road out of sight that he visibly relaxes. I wipe away his tears. He grabs me and pulls me so tight to him I can barely breathe. It's as if he's holding on to me for dear life.

"Dylan, please, talk to me. What's going on?"

"Anni, you won't understand." He chokes on his words.

"What do you mean? Try me. I'm here for you."

Dylan shakes his head.

"I gotta go," he announces.

"What? Go where?" I ask.

"For a walk. Out. Something." He reaches for the hoodie on the kitchen chair and swings it over his shoulders, his arms slipping in easily.

"Can I come?" I ask. What if the bear is still milling around?

"No. You stay here. You need to rest."

"You just got back!"

Dylan kisses me softly on the forehead before heading out. I stand in one spot, watching as he checks for traffic on the gravel road before darting across. He heads toward the forest, and I wonder if he knows where he's going. I rub my arms and try not to worry — after all, I bet Dylan knows this beautiful forest pretty well.

I perch on the end of the blue chair in the corner, where I have a view of both the door and the front window — that way I can watch for Dylan when he returns. It strikes me again that nothing is going how I thought it would. It makes me think of my family back home, and at this moment I miss them.

I reach for my phone, wondering if my mom has texted, but my pocket is empty. I pat my other pockets and look on the coffee table, but my phone isn't there either. Maybe I left it upstairs when I was sleeping.

The sound of tires on gravel snaps my attention back to the window. My heart starts to pound when I see that it's the RCMP car pulling into the driveway. A tall officer in uniform gets out and glances into the fire pit before looking around. He's about my dad's age, and even though he's wearing a hat I imagine that he's balding like my dad, too.

He walks onto the deck and knocks on the front door. The knock is loud and strong, and I shake a little as I rush to the door. I pull it open.

"Good afternoon," the police officer says. His tone is matter-of-fact.

"Hello," I stammer. I read his nametag: Cst. Merell.

"Who is staying here at the moment?" he asks. I pull my sweater tighter around me, hoping to keep the cold air from making me shiver.

"I'm here with my boyfriend's family," I say. "This is their cabin."

I realize that I'm not completely telling the truth here, but I don't want to draw suspicion about two teenagers up here alone.

"Are you looking for the bear?" I ask, hoping to find out why he's here.

"What bear is that?" The officer raises his eyebrows.

"There was one roaming around. Earlier today."

"First I heard of it," the officer says. "But I can take a look around and put out a warning."

We stand awkwardly at the doorway. If he's not here about the bear, what is he here for?

"Are Kathy and Ed here?"

I almost jump at his words. He knows Dylan's parents personally? But, wait, isn't Dylan's dad's name Allan? My heart starts thudding in my chest. I wonder if he can sense my sudden fear.

"Of course," I reply. "Just out for a walk. I'm surprised you didn't see them!"

I realize that I'm starting to spin quite the tale and that this could really get me in trouble, but he must not find out that Dylan and I are here alone.

"Hear anything funny this afternoon?"

"Funny?" I stutter. "Like what?"

"Gunshots?"

"Gunshots?!"

"Someone was caught hunting right here at this beach — right here on private property, but close to our public trails ..." Cst. Merell shakes his head. "Could've killed someone. Not to mention that hunting on that land is illegal."

I feel the colour drain from my face. Is he looking for Dylan, then? This is about the hunt and not about some bear? I suddenly feel sick to my stomach. No wonder Dylan freaked out when he saw the police car. Now I know why he got out of here so quickly.

"Sorry, I can't help you there. I wasn't feeling well. I was napping." I hope my quivering lips and legs don't give me away. I feel as though my knees are knocking together now.

"Okay, well, you have a nice weekend now," Cst. Merell says. He turns to head back down the deck stairs to his car but then looks back at me and says, "Say hi to Peter for me, too!"

I nod and shut the door carefully. Who the heck is Peter?

DYLAN

I'm hunched beneath a fallen tree trunk and some shrubbery. I don't hear any sounds but the odd chitter-chatter of a squirrel, the wind whistling through the trees, and the singing of birds. I just need some time to sit here and think. Time to think of what I'm going to do next and how I can get us out of this mess. What if the RCMP start asking around about who is up here right now? What if Annika is questioned? What will she say? All I can think is how we've barely gotten up here and already it feels like it is game over. I rest my head up against the rough bark of the fallen tree and nestle into the soft moss below me.

I miss my mom. I wish I hadn't lied about her to Annika. I wish they could meet and be friends and that I could see her right now. I think of how angry I feel toward her but how I'd do anything to feel her arms around me at this moment, consoling me and assuring me that everything will be okay. I think of how often I push her away and I am flooded with regret.

Crouching in this area brings back a memory. I try to fight it, knowing that it's not one that I want to remember, but it plays like a reel inside my head. I squeeze my eyes shut, as though that will keep it from getting to the surface, but it flashes through my mind like a wildfire.

I am eleven years old. We are up here at the cabin. My family and the Johnsons, a family we know from basketball. Their son Jared and I are the same age. We played minor league basketball together for many years. Jared's parents, Joe and Samantha, are about the same age as my parents. Once they met they became fast friends. They came to stay with us at our cabin many times. Jared and I loved it because we could spend entire weekends together. We'd fish and swim at the beach. We even fashioned a basketball net out of rebar that my dad bent for us and tried playing basketball on the forest floor. That one summer, we were riding our bikes through the paths (not too far from where I'm lying right now), and trying to see who could get back to the cabin faster. We were both flying, our mountain bike tires sailing over the rough, root-strewn path as though it were nothing. Then we heard a big popping sound and Jared came to an almost immediate stop. His front tire had blown. Rather than stop, I took it as my opportunity to win the race. He called after me but I tore off, eager to get to the cabin first so that I could rub it in when he showed up walking his bike way later.

I pedalled hard even though I knew that there was no need. Clearly I would reach the cabin first. I chuckled out loud as I rode. It was going to be hilarious when Jared got back with his bike. I dumped my bike onto the driveway and walked up to the cabin, my eyes bright with triumph. I waited on the deck but he was taking forever, so I headed into the cabin, thinking I'd get a drink.

When I walked in, the cabin was quiet. I grabbed a glass from the cabinet and filled it at the water cooler. I stood over the sink to drink it. While I was drinking I glanced out the back window. It took a moment for my eyes to adjust, but when they did, the glass fell from my fingers and smashed against the stainless steel sink.

My dad and Samantha, Jared's mom, were locked in a tight embrace. They were kissing passionately, their mouths and tongues moving madly, and my dad had his hands up her shirt. They were behind the cabin, obviously thinking they were out of view, but I was close enough to know what I was seeing. My hand flew to my mouth.

Where's Mom? I thought. *She* has *to see this. She has to know.* But then I thought of my mother finding out, and the thought just about killed me. *How could he hurt her like this?* I wanted to run out and punch my dad. I wanted to rip Samantha away from him and shake her. *What about your husband? What about your son?* I wanted to scream at her.

Then I heard my mom's voice from upstairs.

"Dylan? Is that you?" she called out.

"Yes, Mom! It's okay. Just stay upstairs."

"Did something break?"

"I got it, Mom. Don't worry!" The last thing I needed was my mom coming down and seeing this. If she was upstairs all she'd have to do is glance out the bedroom window and downward to see them. They were lucky she hadn't caught it already. Plus where was Joe, Jared's dad?

Jared would be back soon, too. There's no way I could let him see his mom making out with my dad. I ran back outside and started calling for my dad, knowing that it would put a quick end to their make-out session.

Sure enough, my dad came around the corner whistling, as though nothing was out of the ordinary. He was carrying some logs as though he'd been collecting wood all along. He smiled at me and asked where Jared was.

"Where's Samantha?" I asked him point blank. Dad gave me a funny little smile and shrugged. "I'm sure she's around here somewhere," he said.

"Yes, I'm sure she is," I said back. Dad paused to look at me. He knew that I knew. I looked daggers at him.

"Now son," he rushed to me. "Whatever you think you saw …"

"I know what I saw," I spat at him. "Does Mom know?"

Dad dropped the wood at his feet and pulled at his collar.

"Does Mom know?" I repeated.

His face was ashen. He tried to put his arm around me, but I bailed. I turned and fled as fast as my legs would take me and I ran straight back toward the woods. Once I got onto the gravel road, I saw Jared practically limping his bike back to the cabin.

"The least you could do is help me," Jared yelled at me. "Thanks a lot for just leaving me there!"

I wanted to stop. I wanted to help him. I wanted to beg him not to go back to that cabin so that there would never be a chance that he'd find out about my dad and his mom. I wanted to protect him from the pain that was searing through my gut and my heart at that moment. But I couldn't. All I wanted to do was run away and hide it somewhere deep inside where it would never resurface, where he'd never have the chance to find out. So I did what I knew how to do best. I ran. I ran and threw myself down onto the ground and cried. I cried until my whole body was worn and tired. I took twigs and snapped them in my hands, grateful to unleash my anger onto something. The snap of the wood made me feel good — like if I could just break something, something else could deal with the pain so that I wouldn't have to.

Having that memory flood up so many years later makes me realize that by burying the pain, I haven't gotten any closer to healing. Instead, it flashes through my mind as though it's happening in real time all over again. I put my head in my hands and start to cry again. This time they are the tears of a young adult, not the young child I once was. But the pain isn't any less strong all these years later.

6:00 P.M.

ANNIKA

I've searched this cabin high and low for my phone and I can't find it anywhere. How could it have just disappeared? I was sure I had it in my pocket. And Dylan still isn't back. It's really dark out already. What will I do if he doesn't come home?

I can't even call him. He's left his phone here at the cabin. It's sitting on the table, taunting me since I can't find mine. That means he has no way to reach me, either. Where could he be? Is he out in the woods? Even if he went for a long walk, he should have been back by now. I mean, he doesn't even have a flashlight with him. Did the RCMP officer see him? And what then?

Dylan's story about the bear seems a lot less plausible now that I've heard about the hunting incident. As smart as I know Dylan is about hunting, it wouldn't surprise me that he'd do things his way. *But would his way include doing something illegal?* I don't want to believe that, but suddenly I'm not sure, remembering how he came running back, wild-eyed and sweaty, trying to usher me into the cabin as fast as he could. *What really happened out there?*

Dylan's phone starts pinging, and I know he's receiving texts. I have never been on his phone without his permission, and I don't intend to start, until something nags at me to pick it up. It's his mom.

Can you call me Dylan? We're looking for you. 6:12 p.m.

You and me both, I want to say. Then it dawns on me that they should know where we are. Dylan said himself he told them we were coming up. That's how he got the key.

It's important. 6:12 p.m.

Uh oh. Something important? What do I do? I decide to text her back.

Mrs. Sopick, it's Annika. Dylan is just out right now. I'll let him know u called. 6:13 p.m.

Thanks, Annika. Is he at your house? 6:13 p.m.

No. We r at your cabin. 6:14 p.m.

What cabin? 6:14 p.m.

What does she mean "what cabin?"

Your cabin. At Delaronde. 6:15 p.m.

There is a long pause.

We don't have a cabin at Delaronde. At least not anymore. 6:20 p.m.

What? 6:21 p.m.

It's a stupid thing to type but I don't know what else to say.

We sold our cabin years ago. 6:21 p.m.

Dylan's phone starts ringing and I know without a doubt that it's his mom, obviously trying to figure out what is going on. I can't answer it. I can't do it. I switch the phone to vibrate to try to quell my nerves. My stomach flops wildly. My mouth goes dry. How can this be true? Whose cabin are we in? Did Dylan lie about this?

Looking around at the cabin now gives me shivers. Am I trespassing onto someone else's property? This can't be happening. As though I need something to convince me otherwise, I put down Dylan's phone and start rummaging through drawers, hoping for something to reassure me that there's been a misunderstanding, that there is indeed a cabin here that his parents own. Maybe his dad owns it but his mom doesn't know about it. Yes. That's it. If she lives across the country, there may be a cabin she knows nothing about.

Dylan's dad owns it then. 6:27 p.m.

I'm pretty sure if he owned property, as his wife, I'd know about it. 6:29 p.m.

Another bombshell. Married? Dylan told me his parents were divorced and that his mom had remarried and lived across the country. I keep rummaging through things, hoping for a sign of some sort. I flip open a hardcover notebook that says "Phone" on the front. A square of paper is taped in the inside cover. It reads: Kathy and Ed Iverson, 306-469-0298, Lot 14, Block 5. Seeing their names makes my heart thump harder than I've ever heard it. These are the same names the RCMP officer used. My cheeks flush with fear. I am quite possibly standing in a stranger's cabin, having trespassed. There's no way Dylan would bring us here if it no longer belonged to his family, would he? It doesn't make sense. He has stories about this place. Some of his family's things are still here. I try to make sense of things but nothing seems to add up no matter how I try to look at it. What if the RCMP officer comes back? What if he realizes we shouldn't be here and we're arrested? My stomach twists so tightly I want to double over.

Then Dylan's phone buzzes, and I know it's his mom trying to call again. This time I press talk, and put the phone to my ear.

"Hello?"

"Annika, this is Anna. I know we've never met, but I've heard lovely things about you from Allan. He says you are darling," Dylan's mom starts. I am silent. "Now tell me, where are you again?"

"We're at Delaronde. Dylan brought us here." My voice trails off. I have no idea what is happening at this moment.

"Oh, honey, we sold that cabin years ago. We didn't have the time to use it anymore. You must be staying somewhere else?"

"No. Dylan showed me the bench he made. The walls his dad put up. It has to be …"

"What does it look like, dear?" she says gently.

I'm numb. "It's a one-and-a-half-storey. With log siding."

Dylan's mom lets out a gasp.

"Oh Dylan … what have you done?" she says. "Annika, listen to me. Do you know where he is?"

"No. He was upset. He left about an hour ago and he hasn't come back."

"Does he have his medication with him?"

"His medication? I'm not sure. What medication does he take?"

"Listen, Annika, I don't mean to scare you, but you aren't supposed to be there right now. I mean it when we say that we no longer own a cabin there. And for Dylan, you need to find out if he has his medication. Do you hear me? It's very important that he takes his medication."

"Is he sick?" I ask.

"He needs that medication. He hasn't wanted to take his medication the past few months, but he has to!"

I wonder if Dylan has been taking his meds. Then it occurs to me to wonder if his mood swings play any part in this illness. Suddenly I don't know what's real or what's not.

"You need to find him, Annika. And Allan and I, we'll call the police and make our way up there, okay?"

"No!" I say quickly. "You can't do that. Dylan will freak out."

"Annika, we have to. Something is really wrong here and we have to figure out what's going on."

Suddenly I want to throw up. I want to turn back the clock so that I never heard any of this. I want to set this phone down on the table because if I could go back in time, I wouldn't pick it up.

DYLAN

It's starting to get pretty dark as I step onto the gravel road from the forest. It's a combination of the dark storm clouds that have rolled in and the night sky settling in as it does each day. My bones feel weary — achy, throbbing, almost brittle. I feel like I'm a smashed version of myself. Fragmented and badly put back together. I may crack and shatter again. Broken pieces. What if this next time I can't be put back together again?

All I want is to go back to the cabin and embrace Annika. I want to feel her love and her arms around me. I need to hear that everything is going to be okay. I need her to reassure me that we're going to be fine.

The cabin comes into view. Just the sight of the front of it fills me with a joy I've been missing for so long. It reminds me of happier times, times when our family was a solid unit, before everything started falling apart. I never wanted to say goodbye to this place. I didn't want to believe that our time here was coming to an end. It feels so good to be here, enjoying what I feel is still rightfully ours. It should never have been sold.

When I swing open the door to the cabin, I expect to see Annika. I listen for a moment and figure out that she's upstairs. I pick up my phone from the table and then run up the stairs, eager to see her. When I get to the top, I see her standing over her bag, folding clothes.

"What are you doing?"

She jumps, and clutches her sweater to herself protectively.

"Packing." Annika says softly.

Surely I've heard her wrong.

"Annika?"

She continues packing as though I'm not even there.

"What are you doing?" I repeat. I yank her by the arm. She yelps and pulls away from me.

"Aw, c'mon. I didn't mean to hurt you," I say. She's staring at me as though I'm some kind of monster. She still won't talk to me, and her silence is making my blood pressure rise by the minute.

"Annika!" I yell. She slinks down onto the bed and looks up at me, her eyes as big and round and fearful as I've ever seen them. She is looking past me through the doorway, as though she's plotting a way to get past me. I can see her calculating her next move.

I decide to stay right where I am. If she wants to get through the door, she'll have to get past me first.

"Why did you say this was your cabin?" she asks finally.

The hairs stand up on the back of my neck.

"It is my cabin."

She looks at me pointedly. "Dyl, I know it's not your cabin."

I remind her of the bench, the tongue-and-groove interior panelling, the room that was mine growing up. How else would I know these things?

"Your mom told me it was sold years ago." Annika's voice breaks when she says this.

"My mom?! What the hell are you doing talking to my mom?" How could this girl I've loved so much betray me like this and talk to my mom without me knowing about it?

"She was trying to get ahold of you when you were gone. We started texting and then she phoned. She said it was important."

I laugh. A bitter, loud laugh. A laugh to signal that the world is indeed conspiring against me. Of course something like this would happen when I'm gone.

"You lied," Annika says matter-of-factly. "You brought me all the way out here making me believe we could have a future together here. But how? This isn't ours to have!" Annika is trying to remain composed, but I can see that she's starting to shake.

"How long was this going to go on before we would've been found out? What would have happened then?"

I continue to laugh and shake my head.

"And what happened today when you were hunting? The police came here, Dylan. And they didn't know anything about a roaming bear. Only about some hunting incident."

So my girl is going to believe some punk stranger RCMP officer over the guy she loves? Nice.

"I'm going," she finishes.

"Going where?"

"Home."

"Oh no you're not," I tell her. "You're staying right here."

"Dylan, your parents are on their way. For all I know, the police might be on their way, too."

The mention of both the police and my parents coming makes me itch. I take a moment to digest what she is saying and then I start to pace back and forth. I replay what she is saying over and over again, hoping that I'll find the answer of what to do next. Nothing is going like it should, and Annika wants to go home. We can't go home. We're supposed to make our home here for as long as we can. How can this be coming apart? My fear of Annika leaving me is coming true and I can't let it happen. I can't. She picks up her bag and moves toward me. I put my arms out and push her back. I push her a little more strongly than I intend, and she yelps as she flies back onto the bed.

I see the fear in her eyes, and, for a moment, I feel satisfaction. I want to be the one to control what happens here, and in order for us to be together Annika must remain with me. But then I see her eyes and I want to take it back. I don't want to hurt her. I love her more than anything. I just need her to stay. We can talk this out.

"Dylan, please." Annika starts to sob.

"Baby, just let me explain," I plead. "And we'll get this all sorted out."

"There's nothing to sort out, Dylan. I just want to go home now."

A loud crack of thunder sounds out, and the storm sounds so close that the cabin seems to vibrate. We both jump at the unexpected sound. Annika's eyes are darting around the room as though she's looking for something. I remember her phone, tucked deep into the back of the couch. She must not have found it yet. I wonder if she's made calls with mine. I press to see my call history but I only see my parents' number. *Good*, I think to myself. *Her mother still has no idea where she is.* I can't let her find that phone. I have to find a way to keep Annika here with me. It's not time for her to go home. She's all I have in this world. I can't even think about losing her. Thunder rolls again and lightning flashes through the window, casting a flash of white across the room.

I know how much Annika hates storms. She wouldn't dare try to venture out of here in weather like this. I watch her clutch her bag close to herself as though she's hugging it. She starts coughing again. She's exhausted. If she leaves, she won't get far in her condition.

"Dylan, can you come here?" she says softly. I smile and sit beside her. *Good, she's changed her mind. She sees how much she needs me.* I put my arm around her and rub her back gently, just like she likes. I want to calm and soothe her.

She leans into me and sighs and I relax, too, knowing that I can turn this around for us.

We lean back onto the bed and Annika nestles into my shoulder and chest. I wrap my arm around her. I can smell her strawberry-scented hair; it cascades across my arm. She's warm and comfortable, and immediately I feel my blood pressure lowering. We don't say anything; we just lie side-by-side, breathing deeply, our chests rising and falling in unison when we breathe.

7:00 P.M.

ANNIKA

As I nestle into Dylan, hot tears cascade down my cheeks. I'm so scared right now. If I lie here with Dylan, I may be able to calm him down and create an opening to run. I breathe him in, and his lively, sporty, spicy scent makes the tears fall harder. I love the way he smells, the way he's rubbing my back and trying to hold me. It makes me think of all of the wonderful memories we've had, and how I fell so hard for him so fast because he's got such a magical spirit. His fearlessness, his thirst for adventure — there's so much to admire in Dylan.

When he's happy, he is so caring and concerned. He's loyal and devoted. He'll go to the ends of the earth for anyone he loves. Those moments are why I fell in love with him. But I can't deny the darker side of Dylan that emerges. When he's jealous or suspicious, or when he's angry — those times when things get spun out of control so fast I almost don't know what's happened. Those times when I start to feel scared. Scared that he might hurt me. Scared that as much as I know Dylan loves me, he won't listen to anyone or anything in those moments.

His mom's words have had time to seed and take root. They have grown and flowered and added to my understanding of Dylan. They explain things I haven't been able to explain. And yet, there's still so much that I don't know. This is all so confusing, and, because of the lies he's already told, I don't know if Dylan will be honest with me about what he's going through. I need to know the truth, and I need some time and space to digest it all. It doesn't mean I'm running away for good, it just means that I need to figure out what's next.

I continue to breathe him in, and my heart floods with love for him. But I can't stay. I can't be here with him, in this cabin, feeling this kind of fear. As much as I love him, I must go.

I slowly pull my legs out further from him. He doesn't seem to notice. I look up at his face, and his eyes are closed, his long eyelashes resting on his cheeks. In this moment, he looks like an innocent, sweet little boy; there is no evidence of the face of rage he had only minutes before except for how rigid his body feels. But I know leaving won't be easy. Dylan wishes for me to stay here. He believes we can make everything right again. And yes, we could, for a time. But it'd only be a matter of time.

DYLAN

It feels so good to be lying here with my girl in my arms. The rain pelts against the metal roof in loud sheets. I wish it could just be the two of us together forever, right here in this spot — but as much as I want to relax with her, I'm practically vibrating. I think of Annika's words. My parents are on their way here, and the police might be, too. I think of what this means for me. I will be charged with breaking and entering and carted off. My parents will most likely sign something to have me committed into a hospital for treatment since I haven't been taking my medicine. They've been threatening to do it for quite a while now, and that's one of the reasons I wanted to get far from them.

Annika will leave me, because who would stay with a guy who doesn't have anything to offer? Why would she stay with a guy who has to pop pills to keep his head on straight? My mom tells me this is okay, that there's nothing wrong with having to take pills to feel better, and that it's no different than wearing glasses when you need help seeing. But she doesn't know how it feels to be so jumbled and different.

We all know it when other people are sick physically. Everyone talks about that. I don't know anyone else who is feeling sick in their mind. No one talks about it. If there are others, they keep it pretty secret. It's hard not to feel like a freak. Some days I wish I could just keep pretending that nothing is wrong. Other days I wish I knew other people going through this so we could talk about it. I want to know I'm not alone.

I picture my life in a strait jacket in the hospital after this, alone in a sterile, cold, empty room. All alone. I know it's probably not going to be like that in the hospital, but my mind doesn't choose anything kinder to focus on. I picture my mom weeping as she watches me from the little window in the door while my dad tries to console her. But he'll never take away her pain either. The pain she feels about losing her son to an illness she can't take away. The pain she feels knowing that her husband's touch is devoid of any true love because she knows of that time. That woman. And all of the women since.

I picture myself watching the stars late at night; I will always think of wishing on stars with Annika the night of our second date. No other person will ever compare to the beautiful, luminous girl I met so many months ago. I wonder what will be left to live for. My breath catches in my throat at this thought.

And then she's up, and running so quickly down the stairs it takes me a moment to register what she is doing. I jump up after her.

"Annika!" I scream. "Don't go!" She doesn't slow. She doesn't even turn around. I can hear her footsteps on the deck outside before I even make it to the bottom of the steps. I continue to call her name.

When I get outside, the rain is like a grey curtain across the entire landscape. I can barely make out her figure as she runs down the road. I slam the door behind me and race after her.

8:00 P.M.

ANNIKA

If it wasn't for the thunderstorm, he would have found me already. The wind is kicking up everything in its path. At times, I have to shield my face from the debris that flies at me. If it isn't stray twigs and leaves biting at my face, it's the spray of rain and debris that nips at my cheeks. I run with my arms crossed in front of my face, peeking out of the corners of my elbows. My eyes dart around as I try to plot my next move. I have to find cover quickly. My lungs burn, my heart hammers away in my chest, and my breathing is nothing more than a long drawn-out whistle. The wheezing has taken over. My body aches and begs me to stop. It feels as though all of my body's resources have given up the chase and are focusing on helping me gain oxygen instead. I start to feel dizzy, faint even, and I know that I'll have to rest somewhere before I pass out. Otherwise, he will find me.

I try to draw a deep breath, but the air feels thick and muggy, and it is so windy I am sure that the wind itself has dived in and sucked out my breath as I inhale. I begin to cough, a relentless, raspy cough that feels like daggers in my chest. Few people would be crazy enough to be standing outside during this kind of weather. A patio umbrella is rolling across the ground toward the road, clearly ripped from its post, and I almost have to leap over it. The rain is coming down in sheets, almost like a whiteout during a snowstorm. I can barely see anything in front of me, just a haze of grey.

I remember how all of the cabins looked closed up for the season when we were walking to the dock to fish. Where can I find help? It's getting dark, and I just hope that I'll see the glow of lights somewhere.

I fight the urge to vomit now, as bile climbs up my throat. I think about giving up, about curling up into a little ball among the grove of trees along one side of the road. Every part of my body screams at me to stop, but my mind remains steadfast in its mission. It is harder to see the cabins now through the downpour.

Deciding to cut across the road into the trees is risky; I could lose my way easily and become lost. *I'll head into the trees, but I'll still follow the road,* I decide. I marvel at the soft mossy ground cover under my feet, but the uneven ground causes me to stumble even more. The trees provide some cover from the wind and the rain, and I gulp air as deeply as I can. I also get a better view of my surroundings, and I see a path that leads into the forest.

Knowing that the path might not be a great choice for my safety, I think of Dylan looking for me and decide to take the chance. I turn down the path.

Although the sun has long disappeared because of the storm, the increasingly dense forest seems to grow darker with each passing minute. I am running out of time. Rain mixed with sweat drips down my face, stinging the small cuts I got from the debris of the storm. Suddenly, a flash of light streams across the trunks of the trees ahead of me. Instinctively, I run back toward the road, hoping it's a vehicle that I can flag down. The thought of getting into a vehicle with strangers feels scary but at this point all I want is to get away from here.

Sure enough, I hear an engine approach. I turn my head, hoping for a glance of the vehicle. It's smaller than I'd expected. I think it's an ATV but the rain and wind make it almost impossible to tell for sure. It veers off toward the forest and I know it won't be coming down the road anymore. It now follows a path in the forest several yards from me. I gain speed as I head in the same direction. I have to chase it down. I start to yell, my voice coming out in strangled notes. I start waving my arms wildly, hoping that the driver will either hear me or see me somehow. I keep tripping over the forest floor as I attempt to get to the path that the ATV is on.

Even though the ATV is driving slowly, I can't seem to gain any headway. It becomes smaller as it gets farther from me. Loud, strangling sounds drum rhythmically out from my body. My breathing is so ragged, I'm sure that each breath might be my last. It comes in such high-pitched tones, like those of a troubled kitten, that I worry that my breath will give me away before anything else. My lungs and legs burn. I can't take another step. I come to a stop and crumble to the ground. Tears pour down my cheeks again. I place my head flat against the dirt and its unexpected softness against my cheek feels cool and soothing.

I lie there for what feels like an eternity, listening to the sound of the ATV growing fainter. I wait for it to turn around and come back toward me, but it doesn't. No matter how much I want to just lie here and rest, I know I can't stay here in this spot. I push myself back up to my feet. I wonder if I continue on this path if I'll find the driver and the help I'm looking for.

Just a few minutes later, I see a clearing ahead of me. It looks like a well-worn path, and when I get to the clearing, I decide to run across and through to the other side where the forest continues. Perhaps there will be somewhere safe to stop farther ahead. Someplace where Dylan won't find me.

My clothes are soaked through. With the strong wind, I am chilled to the bone. My teeth chatter now, and I feel almost delirious. Despite the cold, I want to shed my clothes. I feel tears roll down my face, hot streams on my wind-blown cheeks. *Please, please let this be it.*

My feet slosh through the mud as I push myself along back through the forest. I don't know how long I've been walking for, but I just continue to put one foot in front of the other, hoping I don't pass out first. The branches slice at me and snap as I push my way through. Then the trees start to thin. I can see moonlight cascading from the sky down onto the grass. The trees open up to a yard, where both a house and a derelict shack stand. I don't see any sign of an ATV. There is a large light suspended off of the side of the house, illuminating just a small circle of light. Just beyond it is pure grey; it's the lake, its whitecaps slamming furiously onto the shore.

I think of heading straight for the house, which has golden light shining through its windows, but realize that I have no idea who lives here. Might they be able to help me? What if I'm not safe here either?

I look back and forth from the house to the little rundown shack. Something tells me to go to the shack, if only for a little while so that I can get my bearings and figure out what to do. It looks so shoddy that I wonder if the storm will take this shack with it. Even in the dark, I can see that the clapboard siding has long lost its paint, and the windows are cracked and so dirty they look like frosted glass. The door itself is rotting and hanging at an angle. I run toward it and I hear a loud bark from not too far away. I get in as fast as I can, hopeful that some guard dog isn't going to give me away or chew me to pieces. The shack is pitch black inside and smells something awful, but I shut the door behind me. I've made it.

I try to regain my breath, but each gasp is raspy and wet and sends me into a relentless coughing fit. I bend over, my hands on my knees supporting my weight and I reel a bit. The musty, thick air works against me. With each cough I see stars, and I'm not sure if I'll be able to remain conscious. I long to open the door and breathe in some fresher air, but the wind howls fiercely outside the walls, and I can't risk being seen. The dog is barking steadily now. It knows I'm here and can most likely hear me coughing.

I put my hand to my forehead. It is slick with sweat. In fact, I notice that my entire body is drenched. And I feel warm. Not the warmth of exerting myself, but the ugly heat of illness, hungry to take over. I try to look around, but it is hard to see much of anything. I can make out shapes of what could be furniture, and a bank of what could be cabinets along the far wall, but beyond that, it is hard to see anything.

Finding anything to help me before daylight is going to be tricky. And that smell. What is that smell — a dead animal? The thought of sharing this space with a rotting animal carcass of some sort makes my skin crawl.

My coughing settles, and I'm able to breathe a bit easier, but for some reason I feel overcome with sleep. My whole body throbs and I know I'm in really poor health. *I should be safe here*, I think. *At least not for now.* My breathing slows, but it still comes out in a rattled wheeze. I wipe my eyes, feeling the hot tears again. The room begins to spin, and my body cries out for rest.

I think of my mom and her concerned face when she fawns over me. I'm normally so irritated by it and I tell her she's being overbearing. Now I'd do anything to have her here. I want to hear her voice and feel her arms around me. I wish I had my phone so that I could call her or text her and let her know how much I need her right now. She'd hear the fear in my voice and realize how sick I sound, and she'd go to the ends of the earth to find me and take care of me. This I know. I want to hear her soothing voice tell me that everything is going to be okay. Standing in the dark in this rickety shed, I'm not sure if it's going to be okay at all.

The same motor sound I heard earlier is in the distance. I listen as it gets closer and closer again. I try to nudge open the door a bit so that I can see out, and sure enough, the same ATV is slowing as it gets closer to the yard. The dog barks with more intensity again, knowing that someone is approaching. The driver cuts the motor and steps off onto the ground.

"Dexter, shut up!" the driver, a large man, calls out. He's talking to the dog but the dog does not stop barking. The man walks out of my line of sight. Then I see him return. He's running back and forth — it looks like he's securing some of his belongings.

Please don't find me, I think. *Just go back into your house.*

As much as I wanted help, now I just feel fear. I want to hide instead of seek him out.

My heart pounds when I see the dog running loose around his owner. He runs a few circles around him and then bolts toward the shack, straight to where I am hiding. I jump back from the door and crouch down, hoping that I can remain hidden in the dark.

The door swings open and the dog practically leaps inside. He must've watched me come in here.

"Dexter," the man says, but there's hesitance to his voice as though he's trying to figure out why his dog is acting strangely. "No time for this, Dex. We gotta get in the house." The dog is sniffing wildly. He barks again and I startle so badly I cough.

The man steps in himself. "Who's in here?" The voice is hard and gruff, and terrifying. I back slowly toward the wall, my arms outstretched on either side of me.

My mind is racing. I could run for the door and get back outside, but how would I get away? The dog would get me in no time. The man might run after me, and how far would I get in my current state? But what will he do to me if I stay put?

"I said who are you?" He repeats it with more force.

I strain my eyes and ears, hoping to see his silhouette, but all I can hear are the gale force winds battering the sides of the cabin. Am I going delirious in my fevered state? I shake uncontrollably. Even my teeth chatter non-stop. I look at the doorway again. I have to run.

I run alongside the wall closest to the door. Just as I'm about to get to the door the flashlight shines on me. The dog runs to me barking.

I cower from the light. "Please don't hurt me," I whimper.

"What the hell are you doing in here?" the man says. His dog stands by his side.

"Please, I won't do any harm. I just need a place to rest for now," I beg.

"This is no place for a young woman to rest," the man says. "Come inside. We'll get you some tea and something to eat."

"No, you don't understand. My family, they're coming for me," I plead. But then I realize they aren't. They don't even know I'm here. The last time I texted with my mom I made her believe I was with Elise, some random girl I met at a track meet once. The thought of this makes me cry all over again.

"What are you runnin' from?" The man is softening at my tears. So is the dog; he comes to my face and licks it. I stay tucked into myself, unsure of what to do.

"Dear, I'm not going to hurt you," he says gently. "We got to get you inside. My wife will help. We have to get out of this storm and somewhere warm."

"It's okay, I'll head back," I say, though I know I would never make it back now.

"Back where? Is there somewhere I can take you?"

"I'm at … I'm … I'm at a cabin," I manage. "With my boyfriend."

"Okay. I can get you back there, but I think you need to come inside first and get some warm clothes and some food. Maybe we can make some phone calls …"

"But I can't go back," I say, crying.

"Can't go back to your boyfriend, you mean?" The man tries to understand what I'm saying but it's hard when my speech is jumbled and I'm so tired and sick. I nod.

"Okay, we'll keep you safe here." The man sounds close to tears. I gaze up at him but it's hard to see when there's a flashlight shining on me.

Part of me wants to follow him in and get some rest somewhere warm like he's offering, but I'm still scared.

"Please, let me help you," the man says softly. He offers a hand out to me. The dog licks me again. I stare at the man's hand and decide to take it. He pulls me up gently. I waver a bit and he puts his arm under my elbow to help stabilize me and I shuffle out with him. The dog leaps at our feet.

We get out into the open air again and the storm is raging. Lightning lights up the sky in dazzling flashes, and the accompanying thunder practically makes the ground rattle.

The man leads me in the direction of the house. I look ahead to the golden lights and think of how warm and inviting it appears inside. No matter what happens from here, whether or not this man is someone I can trust, I am grateful to be heading toward this building.

"Annika!" There is no mistaking who's calling me. It's Dylan. He's found me.

I freeze and look around. I don't see him. I don't know where he is. The dog starts barking again and is looking into the woods too.

"Is that your boyfriend?" the man asks. I nod.

"Annika!" Dylan yells for me again.

We look all around us but it's dark and the rain doesn't help with visibility.

"Run up to the house," the man instructs. "Just tell my wife I'll be right there. She'll help you."

But I can't seem to move. I don't even know if I'll make it to the house on my own.

The dog takes off toward the trees, barking wildly. Dylan emerges from the trees and the dog stops and growls.

"Dylan!" I don't want him to get hurt by the dog, and I'm shocked that he's here.

"Dexter," the man says and the dog backs off.

"Anni, I'm here for you. Let's go home," Dylan says. As he comes into better view, I see that he's starting toward me. He's got his pistol in his hand. The man steps in front of me protectively at the sight of Dylan's gun. He looks to me to see what he should do. I start to cry again.

"Son, I think you better turn around," the man says.

"I've been worried sick about you, Anni," Dylan continues, ignoring the man.

"Son," the man repeats.

Dylan continues toward us.

"I'll be right back," the man whispers to me. He darts toward his house and I am left alone. Dylan rushes toward me.

The relief in his voice is unmistakable. "Why'd you run off like that?"

"I just want to go home," I sob.

"We'll get you home, Anni. I swear," Dylan says. He sounds so sweet and gentle. I want to believe him, but I'm just not sure. I know how much he wants me to stay.

"I want to go home. But not with you," I tell him.

Dylan bristles at this. "What the hell does that mean? Not with you? What do you think I'm going to do, Anni?" His voice rises with anger.

"Please," I beg.

"What do you take me for?" He is screaming. I can see the veins bulging in his neck and forehead. I know he's not a monster. But when he gets angry like this ... I just don't know what to do.

"No really. What do you think I'm going to do? Shoot you?" Dylan moves the gun out and points it toward me and I gasp.

The man yells from the house. "Stop right there!" We both turn and see the man holding a rifle of his own. He walks slowly toward us with his gun aimed directly at Dylan.

"It's okay," I call out. There's no way Dylan would ever hurt me like that.

"I'm not going to shoot her," Dylan calls out. "It was a joke." He lowers the gun so that it's no longer pointing at me.

"There's nothing funny about a gun, young man." The man doesn't lower his gun as he moves closer to me again.

"You're the one that was hunting out here on my land today," the man says, making the connection. "You're the one we were chasing."

"Had a perfect buck, too," Dylan says proudly. "I didn't hear a thank you for providing you with all that meat since you stole it from me."

"Besides hunting illegally on my land, you were shooting awfully close to what would still be considered a public beach. Someone could've been killed if they'd been walking in the wrong place at the wrong time."

"Good thing I'm an excellent shot, then," Dylan fires back.

"Too bad you talk like a punk though," the man says. "Ain't no fix for personality."

Dylan spits. "You wanna challenge me, old man?"

"No. I just want to get out of this storm, go in and enjoy some supper, and make sure this young lady is taken care of."

"Well, I got this," Dylan says. He moves toward me, but the man steps in front of me so that Dylan can't get close.

"Anni, come on." Dylan looks at me. I realize that no matter what he says, I will not be leaving with Dylan. I will follow this man into his house. It feels safer.

"No, Dyl," I say, shaking.

"You heard her," the man says. He cocks his gun. "Time to go."

"Oh, c'mon. This is ridiculous," Dylan says. He turns slowly on his heels until he makes a full circle. He looks deep in thought. I don't know what he's going to do or say next. He continues to spin slowly.

"Look old man," Dylan says. "Don't make me use this." He bounces the gun in his hand.

"Dylan, no!" I yell. How could he even say that? I don't want to believe that Dylan would be capable of something like that, but he's acting so different I don't know what to think.

"So this is it? You're just going to walk away? From me? From us?" Dylan says.

I don't say anything. I don't know how to answer.

"Just like that, we go from wanting to be together forever and leaving your family to be with me, to you now wanting this to be over?"

"It's not that simple, Dylan." I don't even know if this means it's over. "It just means … you need help."

"So you're going to go ahead and leave me too," Dylan cries. He grabs at his hair with his fist and pulls at it. "The one person I thought wouldn't leave me. No one cares about me. No one. I've got nobody to love *me*. Nobody to care about *me* …"

"I'm so sorry." I'm crying so hard I feel like my head might explode. There's this part of me that wants to run to him and hug him and tell him everything will be okay, but I'm frozen in place.

Dylan starts to spin slowly again on his heels. He stares up at the black sky and allows the rain to cascade down his cheeks with his tears.

"Run to the house, Annika ..." the man instructs. I decide that he's right. I should try and get inside now.

9:00 P.M.

DYLAN

So this is how it's going to end. Annika will not come back with me. She says she wants to go home without me. She wants to walk away from us, from everything we have together. She is going to leave me and abandon me like everyone else in my life: my parents who think I'm sick, my friends who no longer talk to me, and everyone else who misunderstands me.

As I stare up at the night sky, I realize that there is a whole other universe out there. That in this moment I am so infinitely small in the grand scheme of things. Do I even matter? I look down from the sky and see Annika. She is moving, away from the man and toward the house.

The thought of being alone in this life is terrifying. It's the worst possible nightmare I can imagine, and it's one that's about to become my reality. This pain is more than I can bear. More than I can live through. Why can't people love me? Why can't I be loved? How else do I stop the pain?

I picture my mom, her arms coming toward me outstretched like that day years ago, and me pushing her away. "I'm sorry, Mom," I say out loud. "I love you."

ANNIKA

My eyes remain fixed on the house. Dexter, the dog, walks beside me, as though he's providing protection for me as I stagger toward it. I picture myself lying on a soft couch, a blanket draped over me. I picture hot tea and slippers, and medicines for my fever and my asthma. I picture my mom lovingly stroking my forehead and my dad putting on a funny movie for us to watch. I picture Roxy curled into my legs and Mark sitting at the other end of the couch. It is warm and comfortable, and safe.

When I'm about ten feet from the house, the door swings open and I see a woman standing there. She has her hand cupped over her mouth, but she's waving me in, her eyes full of concern. She must be the man's wife. I look at her and manage a smile because the sight of her reaching out to help me is relief like nothing I've experienced before. I know this will be over soon.

Then I hear the gunshot. It is loud and jarring even in this storm. It pierces through the air so distinctly it takes my breath away.

"Dylan!" I scream. And then everything is black.

11:00 P.M.

ANNIKA

Mr. and Mrs. Sopick stand frozen in one spot. The sterile white hospital walls feel cold and unwelcoming. Mrs. Sopick reaches into her brown leather purse and pulls out a tissue. Her tiny hands look so delicate. She is much smaller than I thought she'd be. She has long, dark brown hair that has been carefully straightened and smoothed into a perfect ponytail. There isn't a hair out of place.

Her slender frame is dressed in a cream-coloured wool coat, black pencil pants, and grey ankle boots. She looks elegant and put together. Only her huge brown eyes hint at the terror and sickness she's feeling. She tries to hold herself together even though she wants to yell and rage and throw something. She wants to scream at the top of her lungs and release the pain that has been building for years but will now reach a new threshold she hoped would never become reality.

She looks at her husband and he puts his arm around her waist protectively. He doesn't look back at her. Instead, he's fixated on the plain white analog clock that ticks loudly in this corridor. He watches as the second hand ticks strong and steady; I wonder if he is staring at it because it is dependable and sure. Predictable.

They stand motionless for several minutes. When the doctor comes out of the room, he motions for the two of them to follow him. They move woodenly behind him, robots. I decide to follow, hoping to hear what the doctor has to say. No one tells me to go, so I take that as permission to be there, too.

"Mr. and Mrs. Sopick," the young doctor starts. He has tight curly brown hair and large dark-rimmed glasses. He looks uncomfortable, as though he'd rather be doing anything else at this moment, and this makes me feel terrible. It can't be good news.

"Your son's injuries are extensive. The bullet entered Dylan's left temple. It passed through the left side of his cerebellum, near the base of his brain. We've been able to remove the bullet, which settled at the base of his skull, but it will be another twenty-four hours before we know if Dylan can pull through this or not."

I gasp at the doctor's words. Mrs. Sopick buckles. Her husband quickly tries to help hold her up.

"He's lost a lot of blood. He's in a coma, and we have him on a respirator. The biggest thing right now is trying to control the pressure inside his head. It's the swelling that we have to be most worried about."

"What about the damage to his brain from the bullet?" Mr. Sopick asks.

"At this point, we are unable to determine the extent of the bullet's damage. It may be extensive."

Both of Dylan's parents break down. I slide down to the ground with my back against the wall to digest this information. Dylan may not survive.

"Can we see him?" Mrs. Sopick asks.

The doctor nods. "Of course."

I scramble to my feet and we follow him. When we get into the room, we all sob at the sight of him. There are tubes coming from every direction. His face is barely recognizable through the swelling and bruising, the tape and tubes. His head is wrapped in thick gauze. His mom practically throws herself at him, and weeps into his chest.

"My baby!" she cries out. Her voice is laced with agony and longing.

On the other side of the bed, Dylan's dad takes his son's hand gingerly. I watch them stand over him, and it makes me cry harder.

"How could this happen?" Dylan's mom sobs. "Dylan, we were trying to get you help, we were trying!" She cries openly into his chest. "It wasn't soon enough," she continues.

"We *were* trying, Anna," Dylan's dad reminds her. "We've been trying for years."

"We didn't try hard enough," she snaps back. "We failed him. The system failed him. The whole world failed him. And now we might never get him back!"

Her words hang in the air, threatening to crush the life out of two of them. The words speak a truth they don't want to admit.

I realize how much I don't know. Dylan's description of his family doesn't fit this picture, and I wonder how much of what Dylan's told me is not true, like how his parents are still married after all, and how the cabin is no longer theirs. Why couldn't Dylan tell me the truth? Why was he hiding behind these lies? What kind of pain was he feeling that he had to invent a different reality? Why did he feel like he couldn't be real with me? Maybe if I'd known what was going on with him I could have helped him through this. I think of how we thought we'd be able to build a life together; I see now that it would have crumbled. I think of how much I love him, and now, watching his parents, I see how much they love him too.

You can't see how much they love you? How much we all love you?

I want to take him and shake him and make him see that we are all here because we love him and we want to help him. I want to make him see that this wasn't his only option, and that it's okay to need some help. I want to tell him that we know what an amazing person he is, and if he could just accept some help, he wouldn't have to feel this much pain.

Dylan's dad goes around the bed to his wife and tries to hold her. She accepts his touch but sobs harder. Moving to the opposite side of the bed, I watch them holding each other, his mother pounding her fists on his dad's chest while she cries. Allan looks like he's been gutted. I look down at Dylan, willing him to wake up. I want him to open his eyes and see us standing over him. I no longer want to run. I want to be right here with him. I want him to feel our love. I want to be able to reassure him that we'll help him through whatever lies ahead.

I realize how awkward I feel at this moment, standing with Dylan's parents at his bedside. I should give them some time alone with him, and I'll come and talk with Dylan later. I step back out of the hospital room, eager to find my parents so that I can feel their love and comfort.

I walk back down the hall. The same doctor who spoke to Dylan's parents is now standing in a doorway. I stop behind him, hoping I can ask him where I might find my parents. He turns to leave, and before I can speak to him, I see my parents standing together in the room.

"Mom! Dad!" I call. I run toward them, eager to feel their arms around me. I've never been so happy to see them. But they don't turn to me. They don't move at all.

"Mom?" I say quietly. I stop because I know why they don't move. They are looking down at me, lying in the bed, a sheet pulled up to my neck. My mom is sobbing, her head resting on my dad's chest as they look down at me.

No. No. It can't be.

But I can't mistake it. It *is* me lying in this bed, and there are no tubes. There are no machines beeping for me, no signs of life to be found. I glance down at myself, and I know without a doubt that I am gone, that the bullet I heard was for me first, and that it must've killed me. I flash back to that moment of hearing the shot ring out, and how everything went quiet. How I had almost reached the house until all of a sudden my feet went out from under me and I bounced along the ground. How the woman at the door screamed, how the man ran to me, how the dog was barking, and how another shot rang out. And how Dylan dropped from where he was standing. All I remember is the moonlight casting an eerie glow over the pools of red that stained us both.

I wanted us to have our fairy tale, but not all stories have happy endings.

Some stories end in tragedy.

ALLAN AND ANNA SOPICK

Words cannot describe how it feels to stare down at our son in this way. How blood mats his silky, dark hair like black poison. How he doesn't make a sound because an ugly grey machine is rhythmically pumping air into him to keep him alive.

How we long to hear his voice, so determined and full of life. The thought of possibly never hearing him speak, of never seeing the light dance in his beautiful eyes, is more than we can bear. Thick gauze covers his handsome face, hiding the damage that we're told has been done.

If only we could turn back time. If only we'd known about his plan. Dylan was always full of big plans — to travel the world, to skydive, to save others. Like when he was five years old and met his first home-less person on a trip downtown to buy school clothes. We wanted to rush on by, hoping not to engage the man as he leaned across the brick exterior of the mall. Dylan wriggled from our hands and before we could stop him he was asking the man his name and why he was sitting there. He reached out to shake the man's dirty, calloused hand. Can you imagine? A five-year-old doing that? The man stared back at this beautiful child in surprise. Dylan had this ability to really see people, especially those who seemed to suffer in life. Maybe because he was suffering, too.

Dylan would bring home stray animals all the time. We didn't want to have any pets, but that didn't stop Dylan from trying. "But they need a home!" he'd beg. We'd cart them off to the local shelter, and Dylan would be mad at us for days. Maybe we should have just given in and gotten him a dog. Maybe Dylan knew what he needed more than we did, but we were too blind to see it.

He was our only child, our miracle baby. We'd tried for years, and after many miscarriages, he was the baby who would grow to term and meet us in our arms. We thought our world was complete; we'd been blessed with a gorgeous, charismatic child who lit up a room with his personality.

Then he started getting in trouble at school. And the phone calls from his teachers became more frequent. He grew angry with us, and defiant. We knew a shift was happening. Our marriage wasn't perfect, but we were determined to stay together for Dylan's sake.

We enrolled him in basketball, and he loved it immediately. He was a phenomenal player. We hoped sports would provide him an outlet for his emotions and his energy.

It seemed to work for a while, so we tried to put him into every camp and opportunity that came our way, hoping that it was nourishing him. We were willing to try anything to get our carefree son back, the one who could light up a room.

When we found out he was stealing prescription medications and selling them, we kicked him out, hoping that he'd see how serious this was and that we wouldn't tolerate it. He thought we were abandoning him; we thought we were doing the right thing by setting boundaries. How were we to know that it would only send him deeper as he tried to numb his pain? He was using, too, it turned out. We've always regretted how we handled things. We should've seen his self-medicating as a cry for help, and known that there was something bigger at play, but we were just so angry.

Dylan was retreating into his own world, one where we weren't welcome. He worked hard to shut us out. He was always angry at us and spouting words that stung so badly, it was hard to know what was happening. Nothing we tried seemed to work, and we watched helplessly as he slid further away from us.

We had no idea how bad it really was. When we walked in and found blood dripping from his wrist onto the bathroom floor, and a knife in his other hand, we knew he needed additional help. He was relying on us to find the answers. He needed us to help him get through this.

The backlog of patients waiting to access mental health services was staggering. We saw our family doctor to get a referral to a psychiatrist, and we were told it would be a twelve-month wait. We felt like we didn't have that kind of time. The doctor suggested that he was depressed and put him on an antidepressant. We took him to counselling and he started therapy. We thought that although he probably *was* depressed, his mood swings meant there was more to it than that. We had to wait until we saw the psychiatrist to get the full diagnosis, and to get Dylan on the proper meds. By then, Dylan was so far from us, we felt like we'd failed him.

We convinced him to start the meds, and they were a godsend. It felt like the medication had given us back the son we knew and loved. Dylan was visibly lighter inside, and he started dreaming about the future again; those amazing plans that had always captivated us. We thought we were on the right track, that Dylan was healing and growing stronger.

He met Annika, and we were thrilled that he was dating such a sweet, caring girl. She was like the magic balm he needed for his heart. But Dylan felt that if Annika knew the truth about him, she'd run. He was so scared of losing her, of the fear that she wouldn't understand, that he stopped his medications. We watched as he slid back into the darkness even though he was still fighting for the light.

Then the kids got this plan. This plan to run away, to this place we don't even own anymore, hoping that by getting away from it all, they'd be able to have their happy ending. When we found out what they'd done, we felt sick. Then we learned that the kids were hurt, that they were en route to Saskatoon in an air ambulance — and we had no idea what to think.

This was not the plan we wanted for our son. This was not the plan we dreamed of.

Could this have been avoided if we'd monitored him more closely? If we'd gotten him checked into the hospital? Could we have saved him and Annika from this terrible day?

We'll never know. As parents, you try to do everything you can, follow all the recommendations and advice, hoping that you'll be able to break through ... but we just couldn't reach him. As we stare down at our son's broken body and spirit, there's one thing that makes itself clear ... we'll spend the rest of our lives fighting for those who need the same kind of help. Our kids' lives depend on it.

AUTHOR'S NOTE

It is my wish that a book like this one helps to start a conversation about mental illness. This book has by far been the most difficult to write. I wanted to shed light on this topic in an attempt to further shed the stigma associated with mental illness; it was quite a challenge. Please accept any misrepresentations or errors as mine alone.

My hope was to create a balanced portrayal of what a dating relationship might look like when someone is suffering from untreated mental illness, and how being open and honest allows for both treatment and the proper support from family and friends.

According to the Canadian Mental Health Association, all Canadians are affected by mental illness at some time — either through a family member, a friend, or a colleague. Approximately 10 to 20 percent of youth in Canada are affected by a mental illness or disorder — and this is the single most disabling group of disorders worldwide. Canada has the third highest youth suicide rate in the industrialized world, and only one out of five children who need mental health services receives them. Because mental illness and its effects can have devastating consequences, it is vital that teens gain awareness of mental illness so that they can recognize it in themselves or their loved ones. Mental illness is treatable — and it's important that those affected get help before it's too late.

ACKNOWLEDGEMENTS

I am so grateful to the people who so generously offered their professional opinions to this book, as well as those who shared their personal stories of living with mental illness or living with someone suffering from it. Without your candour and generous sharing, this story would not be what it is.

I can't say thank you enough to Arnold Gosewich or the amazing team at Dundurn Press. To Kirk Howard, Sheila Douglas, Margaret Bryant, Carrie Gleason, Kathryn Lane, and my publicist Jaclyn Hodsdon — you are an incredible team that I'm so thankful to work with. To the art department that designs each of my book covers, you have no idea how much I love them! I am always receiving compliments on the gorgeous covers, and I appreciate all of your hard work and your ability to capture the spirit of each of the books the way that you do! To Jess Shulman, my editor on this project, you are a master! You worked tirelessly to polish and strengthen the book, and I'm so grateful that we got to work together. I hope our paths cross again.

To my reading group, Bev Theriault, Susan McMillan, Danielle Mase, Maria Deutscher, and Marlessa Wesolowski, the books wouldn't be what they are without your feedback and assistance. Also, a special shout-out to Matt Hogan for your willingness to help me out. I look forward to meeting "Matt" in a future book. Thank you!

To Alice Kuipers and Alison Lohans for being so generous with your time and sharing your expertise about a craft we love. You are both incredible writers whom I look up to and consider mentors.

To Kim Grant for the gift of "sister" support, which I'd never before experienced. You are encouraging and sure of me when I'm not sure of myself. Family isn't always blood.

To Tom Deutscher, a true example of courage, strength, and dignity in the face of unspeakable challenge. You are revered by your family for your bravery and your kind, gentle nature.

To Ben, Gracelyn, Ethan, and Kale, you have no idea how much I appreciate the pep talks and time to do this. I know it wasn't easy for you while I wrote the final manuscript. Gracelyn, being able to share the books with you now and have your input during this process is amazing. Our shared love of YA books makes writing them that much more fun.

To my mom — I am so grateful for how much time you put in, offering feedback and helping me hash out all of my questions and ideas. You've been a compass to me on this uncharted journey, and I feel like we reached the destination together on this one. I love you.

DISCUSSION QUESTIONS

1. Annika is so in love with Dylan, she decides to run away with him even if it means leaving her family. If you were Annika, would you make the same choice?

2. Why does Dylan present a different portrayal of his parents than the reality?

3. Annika wasn't aware of Dylan's illness. Were there warning signs over the course of their relationship?

4. Dylan's mom tells him that taking medication for his illness is no different than someone wearing glasses to help them see, and that no one would question that. Do you agree? Why or why not?

5. What is the significance of reading two alternating perspectives? Does reading both Annika's and Dylan's perspectives influence your perception of what takes place in the story?

6. What emotions do you think Dylan is feeling when he finds Annika in the yard at the end of the story?

7. Dylan's parents feel like they weren't able to do enough to save him. His mom says, "We failed him. The system failed him. The whole world failed him." What do you think she means by this?

8. This story involves many different relationships: dating, marriage, family, and friendship. How are each of these relationships affected or impacted by Annika and Dylan's relationship?

9. If Dylan had shared his struggles with Annika, do you think the story might have had a different outcome? Why or why not?

10. Has the book challenged your assumptions or influenced your perceptions about mental illness? If so, how?

WHERE TO FIND HELP

Kids Help Phone
www.kidshelpphone.ca

The Canadian Mental Health Association
www.cmha.ca/mental-health

Teen Mental Health
www.teenmentalhealth.org

The National Institute of Mental Health (U.S.)
www.nimh.nih.gov/index.shtml

Mental Health First Aid Canada
www.mentalhealthfirstaid.ca

Mind Your Mind
www.mindyourmind.ca

Mental Health Commission of Canada
www.mentalhealthcommission.ca

Mood Disorders Society of Canada
www.mooddisorderscanada.ca

ALSO BY KRISTINE SCARROW

If This Is Home

Jayce Loewen has had to take on a lot of responsibility over the years. Her single mom works two jobs and long hours, leaving Jayce in charge of her four-year-old sister most of the time. When her mom is diagnosed with cancer, Jayce decides to track down her long-absent father in the hope that he will be able to make everything okay again.

Looking for her dad was one thing, but when she actually finds him, Jayce is in for a real shock. When everything in her life seems to be going wrong, Jayce has to figure out who her family really is, and how to live with the possibility of losing the person she loves most.

Throwaway Girl

Andy Burton knows a thing or two about survival. Since she was removed from her mother's home and placed in foster care when she was nine, she's had to deal with abuse, hunger, and homelessness. But now that she's eighteen, she's about to leave Haywood House, the group home for girls where she's lived for the past four years, and the closest thing to a real home she's ever known.

Will Andy be able to carve out a better life for herself and find the happiness she is searching for?

dundurn.com   dundurnpress
@dundurnpress   dundurnpress
dundurnpress   info@dundurn.com

FIND US ON NETGALLEY & GOODREADS TOO!

DUNDURN